INDIE AND THE BROTHER'S BEST FRIEND

Novel #2

R. LINDA

INDIE AND THE BROTHER'S BEST FRIEND

Limitless Publishing, LLC
Kailua, HI 96734
www.limitlesspublishing.com

Formatting: Limitless Publishing

ISBN-13: 978-1-64034-302-3
ISBN-10: 1-64034-302-4

DEDICATION

To my grandparents,
I hope I made you proud.
Xo

THEN

Tonight was the night. I knew it. It had to be. I was leaving for university tomorrow and wouldn't be home much for the next three years. It had to be tonight. The moment I had been dreaming about for thirteen years.

My first kiss with the boy from down the street.

Okay, well, not really a boy. He was all man, baby. And he was my older brother's best friend. But dammit, I had been in love with Lincoln Andrews since I was five years old, and I wasn't leaving here without a kiss.

Everything was planned out. My guests were floating around the house listening to music coming from the speakers in the ceiling, and Bailey and Ryder were here with Kenzie, attempting to get her to mingle with people her own age. And I was going to get my first kiss from my one true love for my eighteenth birthday.

We were playing Seven Minutes in Heaven. And my heaven was Linc. I just needed someone else to suggest the game, so it didn't look like I was

1

desperate, even though I was. I'd ever so subtly been spinning an empty beer bottle on the table where I sat with Bailey, Ryder, and Kenzie, hoping someone would get the hint. My brother was here somewhere, and I knew Linc wouldn't be far behind. All I needed was for the game to start and for Linc to want to play, somehow.

Finally, after what felt like forever, I heard someone shout, "Spin the bottle!"

I may have squealed a little. "This is my chance," I said to Bailey.

"For what?"

"I'm going to kiss Linc!" I was practically bouncing on the balls of my feet.

"You are?" She eyed me sceptically. I knew she didn't think I had a chance with Linc, but she was too kind to ever say so.

"Yes. If we get him to play, I'll spin the bottle so it lands on him, and he'll have to kiss me," I whispered so Ryder wouldn't hear. I didn't want him laughing at me, because he would. He found my infatuation with Lincoln amusing and teased me about it every chance he got.

"And what if it lands on Allen or someone other than Linc?"

"It won't. Come on. Let's play," I said confidently, even though that thought had never occurred to me, and tugged on Bailey's hand. Oh my God. What if it did land on Allen, or Justin? I did not want to kiss them. It had to land on Linc.

"Like hell," Ryder growled and pulled her back to him. "She's staying here with me, away from that bottle. Those lips belong to me." He touched her mouth, making me want to throw up from their disgusting gushiness over each other, as well as making me jealous. Why couldn't Linc look at me the way Ryder looked at Bailey, like she was his entire world?

I frowned, turning to see a circle of bodies forming on the floor, and moved to take my spot. My eyes nearly bugged out of my head when I watched Linc stroll into the centre of the circle and place an empty vodka bottle down. "I'll start," he said, staring directly at me, his grey eyes so much darker than I thought.

I glanced over at Bailey, who was staring wide-eyed, with her mouth hanging open in shock. I turned back to see Linc spin the bottle and move back to watch it with intense concentration. Yeah. He was playing. Without me having to beg. He was willingly playing. And he was spinning first. Oh, no. What if the bottle landed on Mariah or Thea? I couldn't handle seeing him take another girl into the office for seven minutes, but maybe that was his plan.

I held my breath as the bottle began to slow down. Kneeling forward to get a closer look, I gasped when it dragged to a stop. Bailey fell to the floor behind me. No, it couldn't be. There was no way.

"Well, go on." She elbowed me because I was frozen in shock. It had landed on me. "Your birthday wish is about to come true," she said low in my ear.

I was still staring at the bottle pointing directly at me when a pair of black boots came into my vision.

I slowly looked up at a pair of jean-clad legs and a black t-shirt that hugged his chest in a lovely way, and Linc stretched out a hand to help me up. He wasn't smiling. In fact, I couldn't tell what his expression was saying. It was blank. Maybe he regretted playing and wished the bottle did land on Thea. I gulped, my throat suddenly dry.

I reached for his hand and stood on shaky legs, wordlessly following him across the room to my father's office. I barely gave Nate a thought as Linc closed the door behind us and locked it, because I knew my brother wouldn't be impressed with us playing the game at all, let alone that I was in here alone with Lincoln. Although I'd like to think he'd rather it be Linc with me than any of the other boys.

Still holding my hand, Linc walked over to my father's desk and sat on the edge. I stopped in front of him, unsure of what to do next. Did I just wrap my arms around his neck and press my lips to his, or should I—?

His hands came to rest on my hips, and I nearly hyperventilated. My hands trembled, and my knees shook with anticipation. I was so nervous, and I didn't know why. It wasn't like we'd never been in a room alone together before or that he hadn't touched me in some way. We'd grown up together. Played together. Ridden bikes together. Swam together. Everything. Even slept together—when we were kids, having campouts in the basement and watching scary movies all night long.

"So, eighteen?" He smiled at me, shaking a sun-bleached lock of hair out of his face. "How does it feel? You're all grown up now."

4

I shrugged. "Feels the same. I've been growing up for a long time, Linc." I wanted to drive home the point that I wasn't the kid he still thought I was.

He huffed out a breath, pulling me slightly closer. "I know."

I lost my footing and stumbled on the rug. Reaching out to steady myself, I grasped his shoulders. We were face to face, even with him sitting on the desk and me still standing between his legs.

"I think I'm going to miss you when you leave," he murmured, more to himself than me.

My heart stuttered in my chest. He was going to miss me. I wanted to do a little happy dance. "I'll be back. For holidays and weekends," I said reassuringly, trying to play it cool when I was anything but. Nothing would keep me from coming home to see him. Nothing.

"Good, because it won't be the same without you here." His mouth turned up in that half smile that made my knees give out. Did I even need to go to university? Couldn't I just stay right here, in this moment? Who needed an education? I didn't want to leave. I wanted to stay home and be closer to Linc. This moment would not be long enough. A thousand moments would not be long enough. Studying was overrated, anyway.

"You can't get rid of me that easily." I dropped my head forward until our foreheads touched. We were so close. Just a fraction more and our mouths would touch. My lips tingled with anticipation. It was really going to happen.

Linc's hands circled around my back, gradually

inching their way up, leaving goose bumps in their wake, until he was cupping my face. His voice was barely a whisper as his lips skimmed mine. "I don't want to get rid of you, Indie."

And then he kissed me. Lincoln Andrews kissed me. Stars clouded my vision, butterflies erupted in my stomach, and I gasped in surprise. This moment was better than I had ever imagined it could be. Our lips moved together perfectly, like they were made to be joined forever. He tilted my head, and his tongue slid between my parted lips and met mine, softly, slowly. I saw fireworks. My heart beat harder in my chest—so hard I was sure he could hear it.

I wanted to keep kissing him. I wanted to touch him, his face, his hair, his back, his—

A thump on the door interrupted us, and Linc pulled back quickly. I missed him already.

"Linc, man. You in there?" Nate called through the door, and Linc stood abruptly with wide eyes. We'd been busted.

Masking his features to one of indifference, he walked over to the door, unlocked it like nothing had happened, and left.

"What the hell, man?" I heard Nate ask. "Seven Minutes in Heaven with my little sister?"

I waited with bated breath, hoping Linc would say what I wanted him to say.

Instead, he laughed. "Nah, come on. As if. It's Indie. We were just talking."

My heart dropped to my stomach as I fought the tears that threatened to spill. Nothing. He lied. Completely. And he didn't even glance back at me once. I didn't know what I was expecting from him. A declaration of love? Shouting from the rooftops that he loved me as much as I loved him? Okay, maybe not. But something. Anything.

Did I mean that little to him?

Tomorrow couldn't come fast enough. I was getting the hell out of this awful town and moving halfway across the country to start university. But even that far wouldn't be far enough away.

I was done with Lincoln Bloody Andrews.

CHAPTER ONE

Indiana

My clothes stuck to my skin the moment we stepped off the plane and onto the tarmac. It was gross. The heat. The sun. The bugs. Humid was an understatement.

"Welcome to paradise," Jack announced, pulling his sunglasses down over his eyes.

I was not looking forward to the next week. Sure, I was happy my parents were renewing their wedding vows. And the break from studying was much needed. Who could say no to an all-expenses paid tropical getaway for me and my friends? All of them. Bailey, Ryder, Jack, even Kenzie was flying out. Kenzie and Ryder's mum were looking after Cole, so she could have a break and come to the wedding.

Even the friend I didn't want to see was here.

The one who was standing just outside the airport with my brother, waiting for us.

The one who broke my heart a million times.

8

The one who reeled me back in over and over with nothing but a smile.

The one who…

Who was I kidding? The one I wanted to see more than anyone else.

I stopped in my tracks, and Jack crashed into my back. "Whoa, baby cakes, how about a little warning?" He grabbed my waist to steady me before I fell flat on my face.

Linc.

He was there, casually leaning against a black rental car and talking with Nate. In his denim shorts, loose-fitting white tank, and black designer sunglasses covering half his face, he looked better than ever. I was really liking the dreadlocks growing in his hair now, and the fair scruff on his face made him seem so much more…manly. My mother would make him shave before the wedding, though. I could guarantee it.

I was frozen to the spot. Bailey stopped beside me and squeezed my hand gently, trying to reassure me, but it only made me more nervous. Jack whistled admiringly in Linc's direction and whispered, "Does he have a brother?"

I couldn't even answer him. I couldn't move. I didn't want to move. This was a bad idea. I should have flown in the night before the wedding and flown out immediately after. It hurt too much to see him. Loving someone who didn't love you back sucked.

Nate saw us first. He pushed off the car and ran straight for me with that big, goofy grin on his face, sweeping me into his arms and spinning around excitedly. He was much taller than I was, so I hung limply in his arms like a ragdoll.

"I've missed you, sis. Glad you made it. Mum was freaking out that you wouldn't come, because you've avoided coming home for so long now." I could hear the disappointment in his voice.

"I missed you too." Guilt coursed through my veins. It was true. I had avoided going home since my second year at university when we returned for Ryder's nephew Cole's birthday, and I found out Linc had a fia...fi...I couldn't even think the word—my brain short-circuited, and I developed a twitch every time I tried.

A girlfriend with a stupid ring on her finger.

He was twenty-two, and that was far too young to marry anyone, but her in particular. She was an idiot. I didn't like her. And I couldn't bear to see him with her all the time, so I'd not been home for over a year, instead choosing to spend holidays with Jack and his family. It was easier that way, kinder on my heart.

Jack was my best friend at university other than Bailey—and Ryder, I guessed, though he pissed me off more than anything. We met at orientation and became friends soon after discovering he and Ryder were sharing a room. And since Ryder and Bailey were always preoccupied with sucking each other's faces off, it left a lot of time for Jack and me to bond. I loved him and all his inappropriateness.

Nate dropped me back to the ground and stepped to the side to make room for Linc, who was suddenly right there with a smile on his face. His hands were clasped and resting on top of his head.

The action caused his t-shirt to ride up enough to reveal tan skin and a very defined lower abdomen I really wanted to trail my...

"What? I don't get a hug, In?" he said, interrupting my fantasy.

I blinked at him a few times and reluctantly stepped forward with the help of an elbow in the back from Ryder, and into Linc's open arms. They wrapped around me tightly, pulling me to his warm, hard body. I breathed him in. He smelled like the beach and coconuts. Damn lifeguard smell.

I took it all back. I did want to see him. And touch him. And hug him. And kiss his stupid, handsome face.

"I've really missed you, In. I'm glad you're here. It's not the same without you," he said quietly in my ear before releasing me all too soon. Couldn't I just wrap my legs around his waist and attach myself to his hip a little longer?

He reached over to shake Ryder's hand in that manly back slap, half-hug thing guys did and gave Bailey a kiss on the cheek before noticing Jack standing directly behind me. They glared at each other. Jack's jaw ticked. He was quite familiar with my Lincoln Andrews obsession, and he was not impressed. Except maybe by his face.

"Hey, man, sorry." Nate stepped forward and introduced himself. "Nate, Indie's brother. This is Linc."

"Hi. Jackson," he replied and held his hand out, his voice sounding much rougher than normal. I guessed he was trying to make a good first impression.

"And you are?" Linc raised an eyebrow in his direction, planting his feet hip width apart and crossing his arms over his chest. I knew that stance all too well. I'd seen it so many times growing up from both Nate and Linc. Their protective, intimidating, "I'm going to hurt you if you mess up" stance.

"Jaaack-suuun," the smartass repeated slowly, as if Linc was stupid. "Indie's boyfriend. Nice to meet you, man. Call me Jack," he said confidently, wrapping an arm around my waist and pulling me close to him. My head dropped, and I closed my eyes and took a deep breath. Why did I bring him with me?

"Ahhh, shit," Ryder said under his breath as Bailey coughed out a laugh, knowing this could only end badly if Jack was involved. He meant well most of the time—unless he was only doing it for his own entertainment, then all hell could break loose. Jack had no filter. He said whatever he was thinking at the time without considering the repercussions. Occasionally, it was funny and worth it, but most of the time it made you cringe and want to hide from embarrassment, like now.

"Boyfriend?" Nate looked back and forth between us, a puzzled expression on his face. I'd told them I was bringing at friend at the last minute, not a boyfriend.

"Umm…surprise." I forced a grin but was sure it looked more like a grimace. What on earth was Jack thinking? He wasn't my boyfriend. Two seconds earlier, he was checking Linc out and wanting to know if he had brother.

12

"Since when?" Linc scoffed, like it was so hard to believe I could ever have a boyfriend. But I guessed that was true. I'd never had a boyfriend. Not because I didn't want one. I did. I just wanted the one who didn't want me. The one who thought of me as a little sister, and I refused to settle for anyone less. Stupid, right?

I met Linc's hard glare. His jaw was clenched, and I was slightly amused by his reaction. He wasn't impressed that Jack was my boyfriend, and that thought sent a thrill through me.

"Oh, about a year now. Yeah, baby cakes?"

"Yep." I beamed up at Jack and snuggled closer to his side, deciding to roll with it for the time being.

I heard Bailey sigh and Ryder mutter something that sounded like, "Here we go again," and I had to stifle a laugh because it was like history repeating itself. Only this time it wasn't Bailey and Ryder fake dating to make someone jealous; it was me and Jack pretending for…reasons unknown. I'd have to ask Jack what he was thinking. Why would he do this? I couldn't very well come out and say we were only joking now. We'd look like fools. We were going to have to act like a couple for the entire week.

Nate and Linc exchanged a look, with Linc nodding the smallest fraction. This would have been completely unnoticed by anyone other than Nate because they had that sort of friendship—they didn't need words, could have an entire conversation with only looks—and by me because I was aware of every move he made when he was around.

Obsessed? No. That was too harsh a word. Made me seem crazy. I preferred the term "enthusiastically invested," because I was very invested in everything that man, with the sudden scowl on his face as he snatched my suitcase off the ground and began stomping over to his car, did.

Nate pointed a finger at Jack. "We're going to have a chat later." And then he turned and walked over to the rental car, some sort of SUV with extra seats to accommodate us all.

Jack looked at me with alarmed eyes for a moment before brushing the fear aside with a wave of the hand. "Meh, he'll love me. Who doesn't, really?"

"Me, right now. What the hell do you think you're doing?"

"Making that handsome specimen over there realise what he's going to lose if he doesn't act soon."

A spark of hope ignited in my stomach. If the fake relationship worked for Bailey and Ryder, making Chace, her ex-boyfriend, insanely jealous, then maybe it would work for me. Maybe pretending to date Jack would make Lincoln so blind with jealousy that he finally saw me for what I'd always been. His. Cheesy, I knew, but true nonetheless.

"And if he doesn't want me that way?" My voice cracked.

"Then he's an idiot and doesn't deserve you. But from the looks he's giving me right now, I'd say you've got nothing to worry about, baby cakes."

CHAPTER TWO

Lincoln

I didn't like him.

He seemed like a dick.

Loud and obnoxious, making jokes that weren't even remotely funny.

She couldn't seriously be dating that guy. I wanted to wipe that smug look off his face when he bragged about them being together for a year. A whole damn year. How did I not know about this? How did Nate not know about it? I hated that we'd drifted so far apart once she left for uni, without even a goodbye, after her birthday.

We'd had a moment, the night of her eighteenth birthday. A moment that I may have planned for a little while. A moment that happened by planting a seed in a kid's mind that Seven Minutes in Heaven would be a great game to play. A moment that came to fruition after spending endless hours mastering how to spin a damn bottle so it stopped where I wanted it to—on Indie. A moment that resulted in

15

Nate nearly walking in on me kissing his sister.

The car ride back to the hotel was loud and full of chatter with Indie and her friends—her three friends, since I refused to think of him as her boyfriend—though I wasn't really listening. I was too busy sending death glares into the rear-view mirror every time Jack uttered something in Indie's ear. I told myself it wasn't jealousy, because it wasn't. I'd been looking out for Indie since we were kids growing up next door to one another. She was Nate's sweet little sister, naïve, innocent, and too trusting. We looked out for her until she left and moved across the country, as far from home as possible. I'd fought every instinct in my body not to pack up and follow her. Doing that would have been suicide.

"When does Kenzie arrive?" Indie twisted in her seat to look at Ryder, who was crammed in the back with all their luggage.

"Tomorrow." In the whole time I'd known him, I came to realise he didn't say a lot unless it was absolutely necessary. I liked that about him. Unlike Jack, who seemed to love the sound of his own voice.

I glanced at the clock on the dashboard and frowned. It'd only been twenty minutes since she strolled out of that airport in those cut-off denim shorts showing off her smooth legs and that oversized black t-shirt that looked like it might have come out of Jack's closet. My grip tightened on the steering wheel. Was it his shirt? *Be cool man. Be cool.* I didn't want to draw any attention to myself, but I seemed to have the attention of a certain pair of stormy blue eyes watching me in the mirror.

I winked, unable to hide my amusement. Damn, did I really wink at Indie? What was I, a teenage boy? Her cheeks reddened, and she ducked her head in embarrassment at being caught. Why was she watching me? I had a feeling she wasn't all too pleased to see me, given that she was hesitant to even say hello for some reason. Maybe she was planning all the ways she could torment me over the next week, but little did she know, just having her here was tormenting enough, and now I had to watch her flaunt her relationship with Jack-ass back there.

Finally, after the longest thirty-minute drive in history, we pulled up at the front of the hotel. I was exhausted and just wanted to get us all checked in. We'd flown in about three hours ago, and rather than heading straight to The Falls Hotel, we stupidly hung around the airport with our luggage and hired a car big enough for all of us. It seemed pointless going to the hotel when we couldn't check in until after 2:00 p.m. It was now 2:08, and I was more than ready to get out of that car and put some distance between Indie and me.

Parking the car to the side, Nate and I ran in to check us all in first, so the valet could park the car, while the others waited outside with their bags.

"Welcome to The Falls. How may I help you?" The pretty little blonde receptionist smiled at Nate, and of course, he went into full suave mode, leaning one elbow on the counter and giving her that grin that never failed. I'd seen it work countless times.

"Hi, we're checking in. We're here for the

Kellerman wedding," he said smoothly while I stood off to the side and tapped the keys on the counter.

"Right, sure." The girl—Jasmine, her name tag read, making me cringe—said, looking flustered as she began typing on the keyboard. Jasmine. Why couldn't I get away from that name? A chill ran up my spine every time I thought about my ex-fiancée with the same name and the same hair as the woman sitting in front of me. "What name?"

"Kellerman, Nate," he said, pointing to himself, making Jasmine blush more. What was wrong with this girl? "And Indie," he continued.

"Uh-huh. Indie is your...wife?" She hesitated, a sour look on her face. I barked out a laugh. *You've got to be kidding me.* Subtlety wasn't this chick's forte.

"No. She's my sister," Nate corrected immediately.

"Oh, okay. Great! That's just perfect," Jasmine chirped. "It's just we have a double room booked, and I thought it would...Never mind. Anyone else?"

"The double room would be for Jones and Mitchell," Nate assured her before gesturing to me. "Lincoln Andrews. And we also need another single room for Jackson Meyer."

"Let me see." Jasmine bit her lip, whether in concentration or seductively, I didn't know, but Nate turned to me and wiggled his eyebrows.

"Batshit crazy, man. It's in the name," I said faintly.

He laughed. "She's all right."

His funeral.

18

"Okay. I have a single room for you, Mr. Kellerman."

"Call me Nate."

I groaned and turned away to look around, but my eyes landed on Indie standing outside, with Jack-ass's arms around her waist, laughing at something he had said.

"Okay, Nate. I have the double for Miss Mitchell and Mr. Jones. Now, with the singles, there appear to have been two adjoining rooms booked. I have managed to secure a regular single room as well. You just need to let me know whether Miss Kellerman, Mr. Andrews, or Mr. Meyer would like the single room. And I'll place the other two in the adjoining rooms."

I stood to attention and turned to face the girl. "Adjoining rooms? They were meant to all be single." Adjoining rooms. No way in hell was I letting Jack have a room attached to Indie's.

"I know, and I'm sorry for that. The adjoining doors can be locked from both sides for privacy. They're usually reserved for families, but as we're very busy this week, it's all I have left to offer. I'd be more than happy to provide free breakfast in the room for those in the adjoining rooms by way of apologising."

"Miss Kellerman and I will take the adjoining rooms," I said quickly before Nate could open his big mouth and put Jack and Indie together.

"You and Indie?" He raised an eyebrow at me.

"Look at them. Do you really want your sister to basically share a room with him for a week?" I pointed out the floor to ceiling windows where Jack

19

was grabbing Indie's ass. I hated the way he touched her. She wasn't a piece of meat. There was no way in hell I was letting them share adjoining rooms. I didn't trust him as far as I could throw him, and I knew Nate would agree.

Nate's eyes narrowed, and his mouth set in a firm line. He turned back to Jasmine. "Lincoln Andrews and Indiana Kellerman would be great. Jackson Meyer can have the standard single."

Atta boy, Nate. He'd lose it if he knew what I was really thinking and why I wanted Indie in the room next to mine.

"Perfect. I'll get your keys."

Jasmine grabbed some plastic cards that looked like credit cards and activated them before placing them in small envelopes with the room number and guest name on them. Looking at the numbers, I couldn't have smiled wider. Things were working out better than I thought. Nate was in room 210. Bailey and Ryder had 212, Jack-ass was in 211. And Indie and I had room 845/6. Six floors above everyone else. We were on our own.

Things were definitely going to come to a head this week. And it would either be a disaster or end the way I hoped, with Jack-ass out of the picture and me finally getting the girl, because…

Hell, I'd been in love with Indiana Kellerman for fifteen damn years.

CHAPTER THREE

Indie

Nate and Linc finally came out with our room keys and handed the valet our ticket. Thank God. All I wanted to do was get to my room and have a cold shower. It was too hot and sticky in this place. I wanted to relax for a while, have a sleep, or watch some television. I needed space. Jack was driving me crazy. He was only trying to help, but I feared it would backfire.

Linc had a fiancée, and as much as I wanted to believe this plan of Jack's would work, I knew deep down it was futile. I wasn't a homewrecker. I didn't want to destroy Linc's relationship. In all honesty, as much as it would hurt, if marrying *her* made him happy, I wished him the best. I would just cut myself off from him completely to save my heart any more pain.

The huge foyer of The Falls Resort took my breath away. My parents really had spared no expense. Sleek and modern with its black marble

21

floors and accents, it didn't fit the image I had of Fiji. We handed our luggage to the porter, who assured us he would take care of it and deliver it to our rooms momentarily, before heading to the elevator bank.

"This place is pretty swish," Jack said as we stepped onto the elevator, with Linc pressing the buttons for floors two and eight. I was on eight and assumed everyone else was too. Was Linc on two alone?

"I can't wait to see our rooms. Too bad they didn't have any more doubles. It sucks we're not together, baby cakes, but that's okay. I don't mind you sneaking into my room at night. Single beds mean we'll be *a lot* closer." Jack was loud enough for the entire elevator to hear.

My face heated up, and I was sure my ears were red, too. He just had to say something like that in front of my brother and Linc, both of whom looked ready to strangle the idiot. Bailey snickered into Ryder's shoulder, finding it hilarious, while he groaned and tilted his head back against the elevator wall, squeezing his eyes shut as though in pain, when really, I knew it was frustration with Jack. Ryder wouldn't interfere. He was waiting for everything to blow up in Jack's face, and then maybe he'd step in and save his friend. Maybe.

"There are no single beds, idiot." Ryder banged his head against the wall.

"There's not? But the room's a single?" Jack stroked his imaginary beard in contemplation.

Ryder ignored him, so Bailey answered his question with a sympathetic smile. She was the only one who had the patience to deal with Jack all the time. She never got annoyed or frustrated with him and was constantly scolding Ryder for being so impatient and rude to him. "Booked and paid for one person to stay in. The beds are full size."

The elevator stopped on two, and I waited for Linc to get off. Instead, he moved to the side and let everyone else out. Jack turned back and looked at me with a pout. "What room are you in?"

"845." I shrugged like it was no big deal that I appeared to be on the same floor as Lincoln. Alone.

"And you?" Jack stared at Linc. His eyes narrowed, nose scrunched, and his lip twitched. I thought he was trying to look intimidating, but he just looked like he smelled something bad. Jack was the least intimidating person I knew. Seriously, Bailey scared me more than Jack did, and that said a lot.

"8—" Linc didn't get to answer because the doors slid closed, and we were off again.

Linc stood across from me, leaning against the wall exactly where Ryder had been moments ago. Lips pinched between his fingers, he stared at me.

I waited for him to speak, but he didn't.

I picked at the invisible lint on my t-shirt.

I looked at the digital number above the door, counting the floors.

He still stared.

Was it hot in here? Maybe the air wasn't working. I fanned myself then ran my fingers through my hair, twisting it and sweeping it off my neck to cool me down.

He still stared, completely quiet.

The elevator was silent except the jazz music playing softly over the speakers. Huh, jazz. It was a pleasant change from the standard classical piano tunes most elevators had. I wondered who thought it would be a clever idea to play classical music in these things. Really? It was as bad as the hold music you got when phoning a business. The jazz was a nice touch. It was soothing and…

Ding.

I thought we'd never get to our floor. My hands were sweating. That was too uncomfortable. I didn't want to ask Linc what room he was in because I didn't need to know. Again, he stepped back and let me out first. Always the gentleman.

I wandered down the hall, following the small chrome signs indicating the room numbers until I found my room.

"This is me," I said.

"So it is. I'll see you at dinner."

"Dinner?" I paused with my fingers grasping the door handle.

"At seven with your parents, downstairs. Want me to come get you?"

Right. My parents. I felt like a complete loser. I hadn't given them even one thought since I stepped off that plane and into Linc's arms. He commanded my attention all the time. He completely consumed my thoughts.

"No, it's fine. I'm sure I'll find it." I pushed open my door, needing to put some distance between us before I combusted into a flaming ball of nerves.

I didn't know what it was this time that made me

so nervous, but things were different. I just couldn't put my finger on it.

Feeling relieved, I closed my eyes, sagged against the wall, and tried to calm my erratic heartbeat. It always went crazy when Linc was around. I couldn't help it, though. For thirteen years, ever since he gave me that teddy bear he'd won by beating Nate at a carnival game, any time Linc was near me, my heart stuttered in my chest.

Opening my eyes, I took in my surroundings. My room was simple, elegant, and...huge. Soft beige carpet covered the floors, and a bamboo four-poster bed with sheer white curtains had the fluffiest white bedding I'd ever seen. It looked like clouds. There was a small sitting room with a white sofa, bamboo coffee table, and large flat-screen TV. But my favourite had to be the bathroom. It was bigger than my bedroom at home, complete with a double shower and hot tub.

I could get very used to staying here for the next week; I wouldn't want to leave. Opening the sliding glass doors, I stepped out onto the balcony I shared with one room next door. The view from up this high was incredible. I could see the entire resort. The pool was directly below, and beyond that, white steps led straight to the beach. The gardens that surrounded the grounds were beautiful, so much greenery and bright-coloured flowers. This place was perfect.

Hearing a knock on the door, I reluctantly made my way back inside and greeted the porter as he delivered my bags. Thanking him, I checked the time and decided to have a shower and freshen up before exploring the resort.

I heaved my bag onto the bed. Weird. I didn't remember it being so heavy when I packed yesterday. I travelled light most of the time; my wardrobe wasn't very extensive because I liked to keep things simple. I didn't do the over the top, girly, floaty, flowery look that Bailey managed to pull off effortlessly. No, I was rather attached to my chucks and t-shirts. It wasn't like I was trying to impress anyone. The only person I wanted to impress had known me too long to even be impressed anymore.

I opened my suitcase and stopped. My fists clenched into balls, and my jaw dropped open. I was going to hunt him down and kill him. What was he thinking? When did he do it?

Grabbing the key to my room, I stormed out and slammed the door behind me.

The elevator ride was much faster on the way down than on the way up. I found Jack's room quickly since it was so close to the elevators. Banging my fist against his door, I waited for him to answer. He had to be in there. Where else could he have gone?

"Jack! Open up. I know you're in there," I shouted.

The sound of a door opening beside me stopped me from yelling any further. "Indie, what are you doing?"

"Where is he?" I asked Bailey, who was peering at me curiously from her room.

"I'm not sure." She opened the door wider for me to enter and called loudly to Ryder, who was outside on the balcony with Nate. "Hey, Jones, do you know where Jack went?"

"No idea." He shook his head and resumed his conversation with Nate.

Panic set in. "He's not going to tell Nate that Jack is gay, is he?"

She laughed. "Of course not. He knows how fake relationships work. He's the leading expert, remember?"

"Okay, good." I couldn't have anyone outing the truth now. It was too late. We were in this for the week, Jack and I. After I killed him, of course.

"What did he do?" Bailey knew immediately Jack was at fault, which wasn't surprising since we'd all lived together for over a year.

"He repacked my bags," I huffed.

"That's all?" She looked like she was trying not to laugh at my reaction.

"I know it might not seem like a big deal, but he took out everything I owned and replaced it with...with girl clothes."

"It can't be that bad."

"Follow me. I'll show you."

Bailey sighed but agreed, only because she wanted to see my room.

"How come you're all the way up here?" Bailey asked as we stepped off the elevator.

"Don't know. Linc's here too somewhere."

"Really?" She raised her eyebrows in surprise, and her mouth twisted into a knowing smile.

"What?"

"Nothing. Just odd that you two have rooms farther away from the rest of us. That's all."

27

"Uh-huh." She didn't need to tell me it was odd. I knew it. It was also exciting that we had more privacy up here and some time to spend catching up without the watchful eyes of my friends. At least until Jasmine showed up.

"You know he's single, right?"

"Wait, what?" I froze in my doorway. He was single? What happened to Jasmine? When did they break up? Why did they break up? Was it his idea or hers? *Oh*, I hoped she didn't break his heart. I had so many thoughts running through my head, and so many questions.

"Nate and Ryder were talking about it before you came down screaming like a banshee. I don't know the details," she said quickly as I shoved open the door and let her inside.

"Whoa, this is a nice room. Look at the view!" Bailey rushed over to my balcony to look out at the beach and pool below, ending all conversation about Jasmine and Linc. "So much better than ours. We're looking out onto the street in front. Wanna trade?"

"As if I'm giving up this room. You're not going to see me until the wedding. I'm spending the entire time in my hot tub." I threw open the bathroom door for her to see.

"Why do you get a hot tub?" She looked around my bathroom in awe.

"We are here for my parents' wedding, aren't we?"

"I guess. Okay, show me what Jack did."

I pointed to the suitcase laying open on the bed. Bailey walked over and had barely glanced at the contents before she burst out laughing.

"He did it. I can't believe he really did it." She bit her fist to stop laughing.

"Re-packed my suitcase with clothes I'd never wear? Yes, he did, and I'm going to kill him."

"They're not that bad, In." She pulled out a scrap of material and held it against her. I raised my eyebrow in disbelief. What was that? A handkerchief?

"This dress is cute. You could totally pull it off." She threw the flimsy navy-blue fabric at my face.

"It covers nothing," I insisted.

"It barely grazes your knee. Stop whining." She dug further into the case and pulled out a pair of brown leather sandals and a matching leather belt. "Perfect."

"What?" I frowned. I didn't wear sandals. I didn't wear dresses. And I certainly didn't wear accessories.

"This is what you are wearing to dinner tonight."

"No." I threw the dress back at her and held my hands up defensively. "Absolutely not. There must be a nice pair of jeans and a top in there."

"There's not," she assured me.

"How do you know?"

"Don't kill me." Bailey placed her hands behind her and rocked back and forth on her feet, feigning an innocent expression.

"What?" I growled.

"I may have sorta given him the idea to replace all your clothes."

"Why?" I whined and stomped my foot. I was not a girly girl. I'd always been more of a tomboy, preferring pants and t-shirts over dresses and pretty things. Came with the territory, growing up with an older brother and his best mate. I'd hated dressing up ever since I started growing boobs and Linc made a joke about me being a real girl when I was twelve. For a while, I tried to flatten my breasts by wrapping cling wrap around my chest.

"Because this is your chance to wow Linc. To show him what's been in front of him this whole time." Her voice softened. "This is your chance to sweep him off his feet."

"Shouldn't he be doing the sweeping?" I smiled at her, the anger I felt at what she and Jack had done easing with the realisation they were only trying to help.

"You've waited fifteen years for him. Time to create your own fairy tale. Now, go take a shower and get dressed. We're going to make Linc lose his mind." She dug around in the suitcase again before turning to me, grinning mischievously and shoving the dress into my hands.

I'd been dismissed.

It might have been the best shower I'd ever had. Feeling refreshed and clean, I stepped out of the bathroom with a positive outlook and a bathrobe wrapped around me.

"Oh my God. Sorry," Bailey almost shouted before the unmistakable sound of a door slamming echoed through the room.

"What was that?" I asked, coming around the corner to see Bailey bright red and leaning against a door I assumed was a cleaning closet or something.

"Why didn't you tell me you and Linc had

adjoining rooms?" She squeezed her eyes. "Oh my God, Ryder is going to kill me."

"What are you talking about?" Adjoining rooms? What?

She pointed over her shoulder at the door she was leaning on. "I just opened the door because, well...I was snooping, and *bam*!" She clapped her hands loudly. "Linc, was standing there shirtless."

"He...huh—What?"

"His room is right through that door." She rushed over to me and dragged me to sit on the bed. "Didn't you know?"

"I had no idea." I bit my lip and stared at the door. "He was shirtless?"

"Yes...and wow! No wonder you sleep with his photo under your pillow." She laughed, falling back onto the bed. "I did not just say that. Ryder is going to kill me."

"Ryder, why?" I laughed.

"Because Linc is one fine piece of eye candy." She giggled again, rolling over to bury her face in the mattress.

"Now you see my problem." I sighed.

"I don't see any problem."

"He looks like that." I waved at the door I really wanted to open and peek through. "And I'm just me. He dates women who look like they belong on the cover of the swimsuit edition of *Sports Illustrated*. There's no way he'd want me. I'm a tomboy and too much like his sister."

"That's rubbish, and you know it. You *were* a tomboy. But as of now, you're going to prove to him you're all woman. Show off those incredible curves I wish I had. He's a guy. He needs things to be spelled out for him, and that is exactly what you're going to do this week."

"You really think it will work?"

"Absolutely. I'd bet you anything he was behind this. Sharing a joint room. I saw the way he looked when Jack announced he was your boyfriend. I thought he was going to blow a gasket. Even Ryder picked up on the tension radiating from him."

"I hope you're right."

CHAPTER FOUR

Linc

Thirty seconds earlier and Bailey would have seen everything. I hadn't even thought to check if the door connecting the two rooms was locked. I didn't know who was more surprised or disappointed, to be honest. Bailey's face turned a nice shade of red, and she looked like she was going to die from embarrassment when she caught me slipping on my shirt. And I couldn't deny I was disappointed it wasn't Indie who had mistakenly walked into my room. I also couldn't deny I'd spent the next twenty minutes with my shirt on and off again, on the off-chance Indie decided to stroll through that door and demand to know why we were sharing and why I hadn't told her. But she never came.

Instead, at seven o'clock, I paused at the door joining our rooms and thought about seeing if she wanted to head downstairs for dinner with me. I was sure she had no idea where to go, but I decided against it. She knew where I was, and if she wanted

33

to walk with me, she would have knocked first. She didn't. So I made my way to the elevators and downstairs alone.

Images of Indie with her arm linked through mine as we walked in together flashed through my mind. Of course, in those flashes, Nate and her parents were totally cool with us as a couple. In those images, Indie's eyes lit up when she saw me. In reality, her eyes seemed to narrow and shoot daggers at me most of the time, and Nate would cut my balls off and feed them to Fang, his pet duck, if I so much as looked at Indie the wrong way.

Couldn't blame him, though. We were both protective of her, just for entirely different reasons. He was her brother. But she was mine. My best friend. My soulmate. All mine. I'd been threatening all the losers she went to school with since I was nine years old. Every time any one of them showed a hint of being interested in her, I shut it down completely. Scared them all off.

No way was I letting little David Miller play kiss-chasey with her when she was six. Told him she had cooties, and he cried, refusing to play with her again. I wanted to be her first kiss.

I hung Stevie Blake's school bag from the top of the flagpole the day he tried to give her a bunch of flowers he'd picked from some old lady's garden on the way to school. I refused to get his bag down until he gave the flowers to another girl, effectively starting their relationship and making him forget all about Indie. I wanted to bring her flowers and see her face light up with a smile that was just for me.

Those were the easy ones. When she got to high

school, things became harder. The day I heard Alex Knowles talking about how nice Indie's ass looked in her jeans, Nate had to stop me from shoving the kid in his locker. But, damn, her ass did look good...in everything.

Then came Matt Marsden. Poor kid. Showed up at her house with chocolates and flowers on Valentine's Day when she was about fifteen. Nate and I were playing basketball in the driveway when he arrived. Scared him off, too. Threatened to tape him to a tree if he so much as looked at Indie again. Kid dropped his gifts on the grass and ran away faster than a hundred-meter sprinter going for gold. I wanted to be her Valentine.

I wanted to be her everything.

But I couldn't.

I couldn't risk twenty-three years of friendship with Nate for a girl. Even if that girl was Indie. Nate was my best friend, and I'd never do that to him. Bros before...No. Not that. That wasn't Indie at all. She was so much more. She was perfect, and she deserved someone who treated her like a queen. But hell if I wasn't going to make life incredibly difficult for each and every guy who tried to be that for her. They were going to have to prove they deserved to be with Indie. So far, no one had been worthy. They all bailed at the first sign of trouble.

Except Jayden, a friend of Ryder's who was supposed to take Indie to prom her final year of high school. He was a fighter. He didn't back down, no matter how much I tried to intimidate him. For a moment, as I stared him down, and he glared back, refusing point blank to ditch Indie on her prom night, I feared I'd met my match, that he would be the one to swoop in and steal Indie from me. But then, suddenly, his face changed. Holding up his hands defensively, he mumbled something that sounded like, "You're him," and walked away.

Indie was devastated. I didn't think I'd ever seen her look so heartbroken. She sat crying on the front steps in her pretty black dress and worn, scuffed, black chucks on her feet—in true Indie style— though it had been a long time since she'd worn something so feminine. I showed up in a suit with flowers for her, because it was always meant to be me who took her to prom. The thought of her dancing in the arms of someone else was like a knife to the chest, and the idea of what went on after prom was like a kick in the guts. Not. Happening.

She'd looked up at me and didn't even try to wipe the tears from her face. That was one of my favourite things about her. She didn't hide her emotions. If she felt it, the entire world knew, and in that moment, I knew I'd screwed up.

"What's wrong with me, Linc?" She sniffed, wiping her nose on the back of her hand.

"What are you talking about?" I sat beside her and tried to mask my expression with a neutral one, but it proved difficult. I knew what was coming next.

"No one wants me. Jayden bailed, like every single guy who's ever been interested. Am I that repulsive?"

My heart ached. I did this to her because I was too selfish to admit my feelings for her, or at the very least back away and let her live her own life on

36

her own terms. I destroyed her confidence because I couldn't handle seeing her with anyone who wasn't me.

"Hey, look at me." I tilted her face up so I could look into those pretty blue eyes that were a raging storm of emotions and heartbreak. "You are perfect. There is nothing wrong with you, Indie. Trust me. All those guys, they were kids. They don't care about anyone but themselves. You deserve only the best," I'd told her truthfully before handing her the flowers and asking her to be my date.

Nate thought I was crazy for even "offering" to take her to prom, laughing his head off and mocking me for attending a high school event when I was twenty years old, but there was nowhere else I wanted to be. There was nowhere else I ever wanted to be but beside her. And the smile she gave me when I asked nearly stopped my heart. I wanted to see that smile forever.

The restaurant in the lobby of the hotel was relatively quiet, considering how busy it was. I scanned the faces of everyone enjoying their meals in search of the Kellerman table, and then I heard her laugh. Loud and obnoxious, completely unfiltered, just like Indie. I followed the sound of her voice and stopped short when I saw Jack sitting beside her with his arm wrapped around her waist, in conversation with Ryder and Nate while Indie chatted excitedly with her parents.

"Oh, Linc, honey, you made it." Leanne Kellerman stood and greeted me with a kiss on the cheek, followed by Nate's dad Steve, who rose and reached out to shake my hand. They were always formal and polite and reminded me so much of my parents. I guessed that was why they got along so well.

"Sorry I'm late." I cleared my throat and glanced at my watch. Late by two minutes. Bailey flicked her eyes to me before quickly lowering her head in embarrassment. I smirked. Indie glared.

"Oh, nonsense, we've only just sat down," Leanne said kindly, looking over my shoulder as the waiter approached with two bottles of wine. Bailey and Indie both reached for a bottle and laughed nervously. What had them so worked up? Chancing a glance at Ryder, he seemed as clueless as everyone why the girls were pouring copious amounts of wine into their glasses. He wasn't giving me threatening looks, so I guessed Bailey hadn't told him she had walked into my room mistakenly, because no doubt he'd be furious with me right now.

"I think we're going to need a couple more bottles," Steve announced, looking at the girls with an amused expression.

Jack whispered something in Indie's ear, and she laughed softly.

I reached for the waiter. "And a whiskey." I was going to need something stronger than wine if I was to endure an entire dinner watching Jack-ass fawn all over my girl in a...dress.

She was wearing a dress. And he had better keep his hands to himself.

CHAPTER FIVE

Indie

I hadn't realised how much I missed everyone until we were all seated at the table having dinner. Pretty sure both my parents teared up when they hugged me too tight, for too long, before gushing over my new boyfriend who they regrettably didn't know about. It made my stomach drop. I was a horrible daughter for lying to them about Jack and for not visiting them for over a year, all because I was jealous that Linc was marrying someone who wasn't me. I could never explain that to them, though, so I made excuses. I told them I had been busy with school and work and, stupidly carrying on the charade, I told them I had gone home to meet Jack's family. It wasn't a lie, but it did fuel the story of Jack being my boyfriend.

Linc kept shooting glances at Jack and me and smirking at Bailey every time she looked in his direction. Knowing how embarrassed she was about walking in on him shirtless, he was having the time of his life tormenting her. Subtly, of course.

Otherwise, he'd face the wrath of Ryder. And even though Linc was two years older and—in my opinion—much more fit, defined, buff, and godly than Ryder, I wasn't convinced Linc stood a chance against a pissed-off Ryder, particularly when it had to do with Bailey. I'd seen him fight enough over the years, and he was quick.

Every time Linc shot Bailey a teasing look or wink, she took a mouthful of wine to hide her embarrassment. Each time Jack touched me in a way a gay best friend shouldn't, I gulped down the fruity alcohol to calm my nerves. Together, Bailey and I consumed enough wine to drown an elephant out of pure discomfort. Admittedly, though, I was a little jealous of the guy Jack would end up with, once he settled down and stopped trying to get into the pants of every guy on campus. He was a sweetheart, kind, caring, and attentive. The perfect boyfriend.

Until he wasn't.

Until he let his inner drama queen shine. The guy was a brilliant actor. If he didn't graduate with honours from his drama and acting degree, there was something wrong.

I reached for the bread basket in the middle of the table, needing to absorb some of the alcohol I guzzled down, when Jack squeezed my leg before wrapping his fingers around my wrist. "Do you really think you should eat that?" he said faintly enough that my parents, who were in deep discussion with each other about the upcoming wedding, wouldn't hear, but everyone else did.

I dropped the bread. Ryder whipped his head

around and stared. Bailey poured more wine.

"You've got a dress you need to fit into for the wedding," Jack said and pinched my stomach.

Did he just call me fat?

Nate raised an eyebrow and tilted his head, studying Jack. And Linc...Linc picked up the knife. Bailey's hand stretched across the table and touched his forearm. A slight shake of her head, warning him not to do anything stupid, or telling him it was okay. Linc paused. His grip stayed on the knife but relaxed somewhat. His eyes travelled to where Bailey's hand was still on his arm, and he gave her a pointed look. She ripped her hand away faster than if she'd been burned.

"Don't want to look like a frumpy old hag at your parents' wedding, do you, baby cakes?" Something in the way his voice softened as he called me baby cakes, and how he gently patted my knee, made me realise he wasn't serious. He didn't think I was fat, and he wasn't being a complete asshole. At least not for real. It was all for show. And I'd expect the one he was putting the show on for was the same one who tightened his grip on the knife in his hand.

Nate kicked his chair out and leaned over the table and hissed quietly in Jack's face, "Outside."

Jack stood with a smile before leaning down and pressing his lips to mine. "Make sure you order a salad." He followed Nate outside while whistling a merry tune.

Ryder groaned, and Bailey smacked her head on the table. Linc's jaw ticked in frustration, his eyes dancing from me to the door as if trying to decide

41

whether to stay with me or give Nate a hand in threatening Jack. The whole overprotective thing.

"You okay, Princess?" he asked, concern etching his features. Princess. He hadn't called me Princess since we were kids and my hair was long, like Rapunzel. I couldn't count the number of times I made him rescue me from the evil witch Nate-alia, who'd locked me in the tallest tower of the...treehouse in our back yard.

"Fine." I smiled, hoping it looked real.

Linc nodded once and stood to follow Nate and Jack outside, hesitating to ask me again if I was okay. "Want me to kick his ass?"

"No, it's fine. Really."

"Okay."

"What is that all about, sweetheart?" My parents gazed down the table at me.

I brushed it off with a wave of my hand. "Oh, you know, just giving Jack the 'you hurt my sister, I'll hurt you' talk. They'll be back in a minute." I forced another smile. I had a feeling I'd be faking a lot of smiles this week. My jaw was already aching.

"Good." My mother seemed satisfied with my answer, looking back at my dad and continuing their conversation. I loved my parents. I really did. And they loved us, but sometimes they were so clueless about everything going on around them. It was like they only had eyes for each other.

"What is Jack doing?" Bailey hissed. "He's being really mean."

"I don't know." I shook my head, trying to work out how calling me fat would make Linc love me.

"He's being the villain," Ryder said.

42

"Well, I agree he's being a jerk, but—" Bailey turned to look at Ryder and stopped when he rolled his eyes.

"What happens when The Joker terrorizes Gotham City?" Ryder asked, giving me a pointed look.

"Batman saves the day?" It was more of a question than an answer to his, but I wasn't sure why we were talking about Batman and The Joker. I was more of a Thor fan.

"Exactly." He nodded and waited for me to catch on. I stared at him. Closing his eyes, he continued, "Jack is The Joker."

"And I'm Gotham City?" I raised my eyebrows. Was he telling me I was the size of a city?

"Bad metaphor, but yes." He bit the corner of his mouth, chewing on his lip ring as he waited for it to sink in.

"Oh!" Bailey clapped her hands a little too loudly, earning a few stares from those at nearby tables. "And Linc is Batman!"

Ryder pinched her chin between his fingers and made her look at him, smiling at her with all the adoration in the world. "And Batman always saves the city and gets the girl," he said before kissing her.

They were gross and over-the-top affectionate, and they didn't have a care in the world who witnessed it. And I wanted something like that.

Was Ryder right? Did Batman always get the girl? Before I had too much time to dwell on it or get my hopes up, the guys returned with Jack, who looked very smug as he sauntered over to me and kissed me hard on the mouth. Nate sat at the table looking relaxed with an amused smile on his face, which was weird. Linc's face was screwed up, and his eyes narrowed on Jack the whole time.

"Sorry, baby cakes," Jack said as he pulled out the chair and took his seat beside me. I inspected him for any wounds or tell-tale signs that he'd been in a fight. Who really knew what Linc and Nate would do if they were mad enough at him for treating me so badly? I was relieved to find him unharmed, though I couldn't guarantee he'd stay that way. We were going to have strong words later, but for now, I was starving and really wanted to eat a whole pizza. By myself.

The waiter chose that moment to come around and take our orders, finally. I waited my turn and listened to everyone else order the most delectable food on the menu, and when the waiter looked at me, Jack cut me off before I could speak. "She'll have a garden salad, hold the dressing." He smiled at the waiter, handing him the menu before discreetly sliding my wine toward him and replacing it with a glass of water.

My teeth clenched as I fought the urge to slam his head into the table, but that would have caused a scene, and I was too hungry and increasingly furious to deal with that drama. I didn't dare look at Nate or Linc. Pinching the bridge of my nose, I sighed and let my head drop. *Don't cause a scene. Don't cause a scene.* I glanced up in time to see Ryder sliding a wine glass my way, with one eyebrow raised, as if challenging Jack to argue with him. No one argued with Ryder.

"You'll thank me later when she hasn't ripped your balls off and fed them to you," Ryder said, making Jack chuckle quietly and nod in agreement.

"Okay, while we wait, I wanted to talk to you all about the wedding on Saturday," my mum said, completely oblivious to the tension emanating from everyone at the table, no thanks to Jack. We all turned to the top of the table and waited for her to continue. "As you know, we're renewing our vows on our twenty-fifth wedding anniversary."

Jack coughed out a laugh and muttered, "Well, duh, that's why we're here." Thankfully, no one heard it but me. And I couldn't argue with him; I was thinking the exact same thing. Trust my mother to make a big speech out of something we already know.

"And this time we want our children to be part of the wedding. You missed our first one, for obvious reasons."

Like not being born.

"But you're here now, and we'd love nothing more than to have Nate and Indie be part of the ceremony this time..." She paused and smiled before setting her sights on Linc. "And, of course, Lincoln, we'd love for you to have a role as well. You're as much our son as Nate."

"Lord knows you eat more of our food than he does," my dad joked.

"Uh, sure. If that's what you want, I'd be happy to." Linc's eyes widened in surprise. He smiled awkwardly and reached for his whiskey glass.

"Great. Okay. Nate will walk me down the aisle. Indie, you'll be my bridesmaid, and Lincoln, dear, we'd like you to be Steve's groomsman," she announced happily. "We have a lot to do before Saturday, so be prepared for some dance lessons and rehearsals for the ceremony and dinner. Otherwise, all this week is yours to relax and have fun."

But all I heard was "dance lessons." My eyes were wide with shock. I didn't dance. I couldn't dance. I was known for having two left feet. Actually, it was more like one foot when I danced because I tended to just hop awkwardly on the spot.

"Yes. You and Lincoln will have a special dance during the reception."

"Pretty sure it's the bride and groom who have the special dance at the wedding, Mrs. K," Linc interjected helpfully, flashing me a giant, eye-crinkling grin. I swooned. Literally swayed in my seat and stared glassy-eyed at him. No more wine for me.

"Cool down, baby cakes." Jack nudged me with his elbow.

"Thank you, Lincoln, for clarifying that," my mother said sarcastically. "Yes, I'm aware it's the bride and groom. We have done this before, you know? But this time, we want you kids to join us for the first dance."

"Uh...guys?" Nate raised his hand awkwardly and cleared his throat. "I walk you down the aisle and hand you off to Dad, then take my seat in the front row. I don't have a dance partner."

"Oh, nonsense. Don't you worry. I have this all sorted out. As long as you show up when you're needed, it'll be fine," she reassured Nate smoothly.

I had a sinking feeling Jack wasn't the only one with a plan this week. There was a glint in my mother's eye. I just wasn't sure what it meant.

CHAPTER SIX

Linc

The moment dinner was over, I was out of my seat, making excuses to get the hell out of there. The seven glasses of whiskey I'd downed barely took the edge off, and Jack was an even bigger ass than I had originally thought. I couldn't understand what she saw in him. He was nothing but rude to her all night. What kind of guy dictated what his girlfriend could eat and wear? I'd bet my car the dress Indie had worn to dinner was because of him. As gorgeous as she looked wearing it, I knew she'd be so much more comfortable in jeans.

I paced my room forty-three times waiting for her to return to her room. I had a plan.

Where was she?

I listened at the door for thirty seconds, hoping she'd have snuck in without me realising. But it was silent.

Where was she?

I checked my watch, tapped the screen to make

48

sure it was working, and brought it to my ear to hear the tick of the second hand.

Where was she?

She had better not be with Jack somewhere alone. I hung my clothes in the closet then colour coordinated them because I had nothing better to do with my time.

Where was she?

I poured a drink and stood on the balcony watching the waves crash against the shore. The sun had long set, the stars were out, and the breeze was warm.

Where was she?

I listened at the door again for any sound of her being back. I heard the television.

She was back.

I made one phone call then rushed into the bathroom for a shower. As soon as I was out, I heard a knock on the door. Pulling my pants on and rubbing the towel through my hair, I opened the door and greeted the guy with the room service cart.

"Thanks, man," I said and tipped him once he brought the food inside. After he left, I pushed the cart through the door between our rooms without even knocking.

"Linc!" she gasped, pausing the television and sitting up on the bed. "What are you doing here?"

"I brought you this. Figured you'd be hungry after not eating much at dinner." I tapped the cart.

"Food?" She bit her lip, her mouth pulling into a grin as she knelt forward and slapped both hands on the bed a few times.

I dragged the cart to the foot of the bed and

climbed on beside her. "We have pizza, steak, chips, and garlic bread." I lifted the silver covers off all the trays.

"No salad?" Indie quirked an eyebrow.

I may have growled, my lip curling in disgust. "No fuckin' salad."

"Good." She reached for the pizza first. "You don't win friends with salad."

I burst out laughing, falling back onto the bed. She was quoting *The Simpsons* to me. I could have a kissed her right in that moment, but common sense prevailed.

She smiled and shoved half the pizza slice in her mouth. The girl could eat. In fact, she could eat more that Nate or I, and the idea that Jack-ass was controlling everything pissed me off. Hence the mini buffet now.

"What are you watching?" I asked, indicating the paused television.

"Nothing, just flicking. Wanna watch a movie with me?"

"Sure." I tried to act like it was no big deal, but it was. Watching movies with Indie—and Nate—in the basement of their house was my favourite thing to do growing up, scary movies, in particular. "Any good horror movies on?"

"You know I don't like horror movies." She groaned through a mouthful of pizza and threw the remote control at me.

"You love them," I argued, knowing how much she hated watching them. She always closed her eyes and blocked her ears through most of the slasher flicks we watched, usually burying her face in my chest to shield herself from seeing something that would give her nightmares. I hated the thought of her being scared, but I lived for those nights where she'd eventually fall asleep in my arms, hiding from the monsters on the screen.

"Whatever. Just know I'm blaming you when I get nightmares." She stabbed her fork at me. "And I'll wake you up in the middle of the night to check under my bed for monsters."

I grinned at her and pushed the room service cart aside. I was counting on it.

I shuffled back on the bed until I was leaning against the headboard.

"What are you doing?" Indie looked over her shoulder at me.

"Getting comfortable. Obviously."

She dropped her fork onto her plate and stood to place it on the cart out of the way before climbing back on the bed beside me. "Shouldn't you put a shirt on or something?"

"Why?" I hadn't even thought about throwing on a shirt after the food arrived. I was in too much of a hurry to see Indie and make sure she was okay after the way Jack-ass treated her. "It's hot, and I never wear one when I go to bed."

"*We* are not going to bed. We are watching a movie," she clarified, her eyes dropping to my bare chest and stomach before flicking straight back up to my face.

"On your bed, so I'm wearing something comfortable. Shouldn't you get changed out of your dress?"

"Oh, uh...yeah, I guess." She stood and lifted

51

her suitcase onto the bed and began rifling through it, a frown forming on her face the longer she searched. "You know what? I'm okay in the dress."

"Indie, get changed. You're going to fall asleep like you always do when we watch movies, and you cannot sleep in that."

"Fine," she huffed, grabbing something out of her case and balling it into a tight wad of material before storming into the bathroom.

Five minutes later, she returned nervously and took my breath away. Damn it. Why did she have to get changed? Her legs looked killer. Smooth and creamy and lean, stretching up to her low-slung black shorts that barely covered the curve of her ass. I gulped, my eyes dragging up her body unhurriedly, taking in every detail from the sharpness of her hipbones, and the thin strip of skin that was exposed below her bright pink cropped pyjama top.

"Kiss my…?" I asked, referring to the black glitter writing that stretched across her chest.

With a playful smile, she turned and gave her hips a little shake. A laugh rumbled from my chest. Where the hell did she get these pyjamas? Plastered right across her butt were giant, glittery, pink lips.

"Is that an invitation?" I asked, unable to take my eyes off her shorts, until she turned around with a scowl on her face. I would happily kiss her there…everywhere.

"Not funny, Linc. It's not my fault. I packed completely different clothes."

"What do you mean?" That got my attention at once. I reached out and pulled her onto the bed beside me. "These aren't yours?"

She shook her head. What the fu...?

"Well, I mean, I guess they are. They're just not what I bought myself." She sighed and took a deep breath. "Jack repacked my bag, replacing all my clothes with...this." She ran her hands down her body, making me wish she'd either put a robe on or take everything off.

I stared at her, trying to choose my words carefully. I knew if I said the wrong thing, she'd get pissed off and likely kick me out of her room. I wasn't ready to leave yet. It'd been so long since I saw her last that I wanted to spend every free minute I could with her, without that idiot around. I was quietly grateful she came back up here alone.

"Look, it doesn't matter. One week, and I'll be home with my own clothes, and things will be back to normal. I can tough it out for a few days," she said when I failed to respond. "Let's just watch this movie."

"Gimme a sec." I jumped off the bed and ran into my room. I pulled out a pair of basketball shorts because they were the only things I had with a drawstring that could be pulled tight enough to fit her waist and took them back to the room. "These might be more you."

She smiled that smile, the one that stopped my heart every time, and ran to the bathroom, only to come back in my shorts. As good as she looked in the tiny black shorts, I liked her better in mine.

"Thanks. So what are we watching?"

"You'll see."

I pressed play and settled back against the

headboard. We were watching *Saw*. Indie sat forward with her legs crossed, watching intently, showing no fear, and I wondered if she wasn't scared of these movies anymore. But then her hands crept up to her mouth, and she began chewing on her fingernails. After she jumped the first time at a scene that wasn't even scary, she was back against the headboard with her hands covering her eyes, peeking through her fingers.

"I hate you," she breathed, turning her head to my shoulder when the creepy puppet-doll thing filled the screen.

"No, you don't." I smiled and lifted my arm to wrap around her shoulder, knowing there was no way she was moving from the position until the movie finished or she fell asleep.

She fell asleep.

CHAPTER SEVEN

Indie

I woke at some point during the night to a light tickling on my skin. I didn't want to open my eyes. The last thing I remembered was burying my face in Linc's shoulder because of that stupid doll with the red cheeks. I wanted to enjoy the moment, bask in the feeling of his fingertips tracing over my skin, breathe in his scent, listen to his heartbeat. Because who knew when I'd get this chance again?

"I know you're awake, Indie," he whispered, and I froze. Well, I wasn't moving anyway, but I held my breath and waited. "I could always tell when you were asleep or just pretending to be. Your breathing changes." He stroked my hair. "Your body tenses, and you tighten your arm around me. Why is that?"

Dammit. He noticed everything. What did I do? Act dumb and still fake being asleep, or admit I was awake and listening to everything he said? Admit he was right. I did tighten my arm around him whenever we found ourselves in this position. Every. Single. Time. Which was surprisingly often. I'd always hold him a little tighter for fear of him leaving or it being the last time he'd let me sleep on his chest. Nate was usually long gone by then. He always bailed early and left Linc and me to watch movies together.

"Is it because you don't want to let me go?" His voice was low, fingers still combing my hair and trailing gentle patterns on my waist. "Or because we only get these stolen moments when everyone else is asleep?"

I didn't answer. I could barely form a coherent thought as I tried to process his words. They had to mean something, but I didn't know what. He was being cryptic. Or he believed I was asleep this time. I tightened my arm a little more and felt Linc shift down on the bed until he was lying flat beside me with my head on his chest.

"I'm not going anywhere. Sleep, Princess," he murmured, placing his hand over mine on his chest.

His heart was beating as fast as mine.

***

The sound of the phone ringing woke me up. Stretching my limbs, I rolled over and realised my bed was empty.

Was last night all a dream?

The phone kept ringing, so I reached over and answered it.

"Indie, sweetheart," my mother's voice echoed down the line. No *good morning*. No *hello*. Nothing

56

but, "I need you and Lincoln to meet me downstairs at nine a.m. We are going to get you both fitted for a suit and dress. Nate is going to pick up Kenzie from the airport with Ryder and Bailey, so he'll meet up with us later."

"Okay." I yawned.

"Do you know where Lincoln is?"

Not anymore. He was with me most of the night but gone now.

"His room, I guess. I don't know. I haven't seen Linc this morning." I frowned and swallowed the lump in my throat. I couldn't have dreamt last night. It was too real.

"I'm right here, Princess." Linc strolled back in with yet another room service cart and a smirk on his lips. "Nice hair."

My hand shot up to my head and tried to smooth out what was no doubt a bird's nest in my hair. "Lincoln is here. I'll tell him now."

"Great. See you soon." With that, she hung up.

"Miss me?" Linc came over to the side of the bed and brushed a strand of hair out of my face.

"Nope. I was asleep." I stood and stretched.

"Looks like it was a good sleep. Come outside. I thought we could eat this on the balcony."

I followed him out. It was warm already, and the sun was barely up. Did I mention I hated hot weather?

"You didn't have to do this." I looked at all the food in the cart. Bacon, eggs, cereal, toast, fruit, juice, coffee. Coffee! I wasn't a morning person until I'd had at least two coffees.

"I didn't," he said simply. He reached for the

coffee pot and poured a cup before handing it to me.

"Oh." I sipped the coffee and tried not to look dejected that he hadn't done this for me. But what did I expect? He came in last night with food because Jack wouldn't let me eat. I didn't really expect him to feed me this morning too, did I?

"The hotel arranged for a free breakfast delivered to our room every morning because they stuffed up and gave us joint rooms by mistake." He shovelled bacon, eggs, tomatoes, and toast onto his plate.

"Mistake." It was all I heard. Our rooms were a mistake.

"Yeah. They were meant to book us singles but had double booked or something. So we were given these."

"Why didn't they put Jack next to me?" It was strange since Jack and I were technically supposed to be in a relationship.

"Beats me. You better eat before we have to leave. Make the most of all this food." He grinned through a mouthful of toast.

He didn't bring breakfast because he wanted to. It was because it was free. My stomach dropped. "Right. Umm, I'm not really hungry, so…" I trailed off, not knowing what else to say. I suddenly felt cold and alone. Which, rationally, I knew was stupid, because things hadn't changed. I was still Indie, Linc's friend's kid sister, and I'd never be any more. But something about last night—movies, dinner, his basketball shorts, sleeping together—gave me a flash of hope, only for him to ruin it this morning. I stood, and before I walked back inside, I said, "You eat, but we need to meet in the lobby at nine a.m."

***

It was nine o'clock, and my mother was nowhere to be seen. Neither was Linc. I sat on the sofa in the lobby, impatiently tapping my silver-sandaled—no thanks to Jack—foot, and waited. I had so many other things I could have been doing this morning rather than waiting in the front of the hotel. Where were they?

Playing with the key card to my room, I decided I'd give them ten minutes. If they didn't show, I'd go for that walk through the hotel grounds that I wanted to do. Explore the island a little. There were meant to be caves and waterfalls nearby that I wanted to visit as well.

"Baby cakes," Jack called across the lobby from the elevator.

"Hey." I stood and walked toward him.

"Your mother couldn't make it, so I'm here instead." He threw his arm around my shoulder and rubbed his knuckles in my hair.

"What? Why?" I shoved him away and tried to smooth out my hair.

"Something came up. Where's lover boy?" He looked over his shoulder and peered around the foyer in search of Linc.

"Not here yet. Let's just go." I turned and began walking toward the door.

"Not so fast, sugar plum. What happened last night?" He reached for the room key in my hand and slipped it into his wallet so I wouldn't lose it. I

59

rarely carried a purse. It was usually just my phone and my credit card.

"I should ask you the same thing. You were out of line last night." I poked him in the chest.

"Me?"

"Yes, you. You called me fat!"

"Oh, baby cakes. You're not fat. You know that. I know that. He knows that. It was all part of the plan."

"What plan?" I folded my arms across my chest and waited.

"I'm sorry for calling you fat. But, look, I might not be your fun-loving, easy-going, life of the party Jack for the next few days. I'll probably be an asshole most of the time we're around him, because he has some sort of saviour complex when it comes to you, and I want to bring it out."

"What?"

"He always has to save you. Protect you. Be your knight in low-slung board shorts."

"Right."

"And I want him to save you...from me, your asshole yet devastatingly good-looking boyfriend who should model underwear or something." Jack walked away a few steps and turned with a hand on the hip, pausing for a moment before strutting back to me. Just like a catwalk model.

I couldn't help it, I laughed. He always knew how to cheer me up.

"Did it work?" Jack bounced on his toes excitedly. "Did he save you?"

"Umm..." Was feeding me the same as saving me? I guessed, maybe if I was starving, which I was. So…

"Tell me about last night." Jack grabbed my arms and made me uncross them. I glared at him, remembering how hungry I had been after dinner. "What happened?"

"Nothing. He fed me because you wouldn't let me eat anything but a salad." I crossed my arms over my chest again and raised an eyebrow.

"Yes. It worked." He pumped his fist in the air. "He came to your rescue with food. See, he couldn't let you go to bed after only eating a salad."

"A salad, Jack? Really? When have you ever known me to eat a salad?" I growled.

"I couldn't resist. You looked like a dying man in the middle of the desert desperately searching for water when they brought out all the food. It was hilarious. Then what happened?"

"No, it wasn't. Then we watched a movie and fell asleep."

"Asleep?"

"Yes."

"That was it? No hanky panky? No tumble in the sheets?"

I shook my head.

"At least tell me he tried to cop a feel?"

I groaned and looked at the roof before levelling him with my gaze. "No. Nothing. Just sleep."

"Well, that's no fun. No wonder you're so grumpy this morning. Come on. Let's go shopping." He linked his fingers through mine and pulled me outside into the blinding sunlight. "By the way, I love you in that dress."

It was sunflower yellow and dropped to below

my knee, but the neckline was a little too revealing for my taste. "I hate it."

"You'll thank me one day. Oh, hey, look, there's lover boy now." Jack lifted his chin, indicating straight ahead. And sure enough, there was Lincoln Bloody Andrews, leaning against a white sports car with his shades pulled down over his eyes, typing away on his phone.

"Let's go shopping!" Jack lifted me up and threw me over his shoulder as he ran down the steps toward Linc.

"Jack! Put me down. Now." I slapped his back. I pinched his sides, but it was useless. He didn't release me until we reached the car.

"Hey, man," he greeted Linc, who only scowled in response. "Let's go. I have things to do this afternoon and don't want to be shopping all day."

Lie. That was a complete lie. All Jack did was shop. He lived for it.

Jack climbed over the door and into the back seat, stretching his arms out wide along the backrest with a grin. "Where are we going?"

"Dress and suit fittings," Linc replied. He opened the door to the passenger side and ushered me in.

"Thanks." I smiled gratefully at him. He was always the gentleman, unlike Jack. I didn't miss the way he eyed my dress. Did he think I looked stupid wearing it? He did give me shorts to wear to bed last night, so I was covered up. He scowled at Jack as he rounded the car and climbed into the driver's seat.

"Okay, so, Mrs K. called this morning when you were in the shower," Linc said, flicking his eyes to

Jack in the rear-view mirror. He was trying to get a reaction out of him, because as far as he knew, Jack didn't know we had adjoining rooms. Not that it mattered, because I locked that door from my side this morning, but Jack just acted clueless. "She said something came up but for us to go to this address and ask for Lavenia. She has my suit and your dress ready for us to try on."

"What about Nate?"

"Nate will go later after he picks up Kenzie from the airport."

"And you, why are you here?" I turned in my seat to look at Jack.

"Like I'd pass up the opportunity to see you trying on clothes." He gave me an exaggerated wink. "Especially if there's enough room for two in the change room."

Shaking my head, I turned back around to the front, taking in the view of the beach on the right as we drove. The island was beautiful. I couldn't wait to dip my feet in the ocean and relax on the sand for the afternoon—I'd go exploring another day.

After only a few minutes, Linc pulled the car up to the front of a different hotel.

"I thought we were going to a bridal shop or something." I frowned in confusion as the valet opened my door and helped me out before taking the keys from Linc.

"No, I said we were getting fitted. And this is where we're meeting Lavenia." He gestured widely at the beautiful hotel.

"So who's this Lavenia chick?" Jack asked as he slipped his hand in mine. I supressed a sigh. This whole "make Linc jealous" idea of Jack's wasn't going to work.

"The wedding planner. She should be here with a dressmaker in case of any alterations." Linc's voice was cool, but his gaze was even colder as he looked at Jack.

"My mother has a wedding planner?"

"Yes. And you'd know all this if you visited or called home more, Indiana." He stalked away, leaving Jack and me to follow. He was pissed. And I was willing to bet it had something to do with me, but I couldn't see what I'd done wrong.

"Ooohhh, someone's a little tense this morning, isn't he?"

"That's Linc." I shrugged. "Get used to it. He runs hot and cold, and I seem to always bring out the worst in him."

"You certainly bring out something in him, baby cakes, but I don't think it's the worst." He wiggled his eyebrows, giving me a suggestive smirk.

"Come on." I tugged him into the foyer, following Linc, who was talking to the concierge.

"Thank you, Marissa." He smiled, and the woman behind the desk blushed. "Room 718. Let's go."

We took the elevator up and were greeted by a tall blonde woman in a white power suit. She exuded confidence, and I felt a little intimidated by her.

"Indiana?" She smiled warmly at me, and I nodded and shook her hand as she welcomed us into the room.

"Hi."

"And you must be Lincoln?" she said to Jack, who was still gripping my hand in his.

"Ah, no. I'm Jackson. But you can call me Jack. Pleased to meet you," he purred, grasping her hand and bringing it to his lips, placing a kiss on her knuckles. I rolled my eyes and ripped my other hand out of his and moved further into the room.

"Oh, I'm sorry. My mistake. Lovely to meet you, Jack," she said a bit breathlessly.

Jack smiled at her and walked over to me with a wink and a little extra pep in his step. Oh, geez.

"Relax, Romeo," I hissed while Lavenia was introducing herself to Linc. I couldn't look at them. If she got all flustered over Jack, I didn't want to see her reaction to Linc. "You don't swing that way."

"Doesn't mean I can't have a little fun."

"This is Serena. She's going to measure and make sure your dress and suit fit perfectly for the wedding on Saturday."

Serena was a small woman. Tiny, in fact. Her head barely grazed my chin, but she smiled brightly as she rushed around the room, producing two garment bags. Handing one to Linc, she ushered him behind a screen and told him to change.

"And this, pretty lady, is yours. If you need help with the back, let me know." She smiled, handing me my dress and pushing me toward the bathroom.

Jack followed me inside and closed the door behind us.

"What are you doing? Get out!"

"Watching you get changed." He hoisted himself onto the marble countertop and swung his legs like a child.

"You are not!" I turned away from him and unzipped the garment bag, revealing the mint green dress my mother had picked out. Why couldn't I have worn a suit? Something like what Lavenia was wearing. I'd totally rock that.

"Okay, fine. I'll help with the back." He smiled smugly when I pulled the dress out to have a look at.

It was beautiful. Something that would look stunning on Bailey, but gorgeous, nonetheless. Long and flowing sheer fabric, a delicate silver belt around the waist, and a low-hanging scoop neck. But it was the back that stole the show, with thin lace straps intricately threaded and woven together, holding the dress in place.

I was going to need Jack's help.

"Turn around." I waved my finger at him.

"Really?"

"Yes, or get out."

He slid off the counter and turned around. Eying him, I cautiously pulled my arms out of the dress I was wearing and was trying to figure out a way to pull my bridesmaid dress on without taking mine off. But it proved near impossible. Biting my lip and hesitating, I slipped my dress off and began pulling the beautiful mint fabric over my head, except it got stuck. The lace straps tangled around my head and wrists in a way I wasn't sure should even be possible. This was why I liked shorts.

"Oh no," I cried.

"What?" Jack's voice was muffled from all the fabric surrounding my head.

"Nothing. I'm fine." I struggled with the dress, trying to detangle myself.

"I can hear you grunting and groaning. What are you doing?"

"I'm stuck." It was useless. I needed Jack's help, otherwise I was going to rip a hole in this dress, and my mother would murder me. No, she'd have me murdered. She couldn't do it herself because it would be too messy. She'd pay someone to do it for her. Maybe Lavenia. I'd bet she could murder someone in the blink of an eye, all that power and confidence.

"I'm turning around, okay?"

"Just don't look." It was stupid, really. Jack was gay, and he'd never look at me that way. Him turning around would be the same as Bailey or that Serena woman helping, but still.

"Kind of impossible, baby cakes," Jack said, and then I heard his breath hitch. Uh-oh. It was bad.

"It's bad, isn't it? Tell me I haven't destroyed the dress."

"Geez, baby cakes. This is what you've been hiding behind all those t-shirts and shorts."

He whistled softly, and I felt him come to stand in front of me. His fingers grazed my wrists and began pulling on the lace, untangling it and freeing my arms.

"What are you talking about?"

"I'm repacking your bag again. And taking everything that isn't lingerie or a swimsuit."

"Don't be stupid." I sighed. "Just help me."

"I am, but I'm kind of enjoying the view here too." He traced his fingers across my stomach.

I slapped his hand away. "You're an idiot. And you're gay."

"Meh, details. I'd totally roll around naked in the sheets with you." He laughed, and my skin heated up in embarrassment. He focused on removing the lace straps from my head. No one had said anything like that to me before, and I didn't know how to respond, so I joked.

"I'll hold you to that. If I'm still single and a—" I paused, unable to say the word. So what if I was still a virgin? "—when I'm thirty, then..."

"Thirty? No way, baby cakes. I'm a patient man, but not that patient. Two years. I'll wait two years for you, and if you're still holding your v-card tight to your chest, I'm cashing in." He finally freed the dress from my hair and pulled it down over my chest. He let it slide to the floor before spinning me on the spot to lace up the back. "But I have a feeling, judging by holes that man out there is glaring through these walls and my back—"

"You don't know he's glaring this way." His fingers tickled the skin on my back as I ran my hands down the front of my dress, smoothing out any creases.

"I do. I can feel it, and judging by that, I don't think you'll need me in two years. Hell, I don't think you'll need me by the end of this week." He winked and positioned me to face the mirror. "There. You look beautiful, doll face."

I blushed again, not used to the compliment, and stared in the mirror, pleasantly surprised at how I looked. I could pull off pretty dresses. Jack kissed me on the cheek and grabbed my hand, dragging me out the door and back to Serena and Lavenia.

I felt like I was in one of those cheesy romance movies Bailey insisted we watch every girls' night in, where a beautiful woman walked into the room and everyone stopped and stared, because that was exactly what happened. All eyes were on me, and I couldn't move. I didn't like the attention. Fidgeting with the neckline of my dress that now seemed too low and revealing, I risked a glance at Linc and about combusted.

I'd never get sick of seeing that man in a suit.

"Wow," I breathed.

Linc shot me a cocky grin. "Wow, yourself. You look gorgeous, Indie," he said, biting his lip and gazing at my gown.

He called me gorgeous.

And he looked at me like Ryder looked at Bailey.

CHAPTER EIGHT

Linc

The dress fitting was a nightmare. The only thing I enjoyed about it was seeing Indie in that dress. She looked incredible. And I may have been more than a little jealous when Jack followed her into the bathroom to "help" her change. I wanted to punch Jack in the face for so many of the comments he made to Indie. He was downright rude and disrespectful, talking to her like she was nothing more than a hot piece of ass. Admittedly, she did look pretty freaking fantastic in that dress. Indie took my breath away. It fit like a glove. Literally. No alterations needed to be made. It was perfect. She was perfect.

But it was like Jack was trying to prove a point, that he had Indie and I didn't. He was over the top with the PDA, and most of the time Indie looked uncomfortable with his advances. Nate would have been livid had he witnessed everything I did. I was sure of it.

70

Finally, after having my pants and jacket sleeves lengthened, we were done for the day.

"Wanna grab some lunch?" Indie asked on our way outside to wait for the car.

Yes, if it was just the two of us. Hell no if Jackass was coming too. The least amount of time I had to spend with that guy, the better. I'd already reached my quota for the day, and it had only been three hours.

"Not for me, baby cakes. I have things to do, places to see, massages to get at the resort in thirty minutes." Jack glanced at his watch before slipping his shades over his eyes with a wide grin.

"Oh," Indie sighed. It might have been my imagination working overtime, but I was sure she looked relieved he said no. Shouldn't she have been upset that he made plans to do something without her? "Linc, wanna grab lunch and explore a little?"

"Sure, Princess." I handed Jack the keys with a smug look, since we were so close to the centre of town and could walk. I couldn't say no to the hopeful expression on her face. Besides, it would give us more time to catch up.

Jack's eyes narrowed on me. "Look after my girl. If she comes back with so much as a scratch on her pretty little face, you're a dead man," he said with a sneer. He wasn't serious? If there was anyone on this island more protective of her, then it was news to me. Not even Nate seemed as concerned as I did most of the time. He'd usually just roll his eyes and tell me do whatever made me feel better about her safety.

But Jack getting all macho and concerned was

almost laughable. The same guy who wouldn't let her eat more than salad for dinner so she didn't gain weight was letting me take his girlfriend out for lunch and to explore a tropical island. It was weird. Either they had the most trusting, open, and honest relationship in the world, or he just didn't give a damn what she did if she looked good doing it.

Hell, if she was my girlfriend, I wouldn't want to let her out of my sight. At least not for a while. I'd want to spend every waking moment with her, catching up on missed times and relishing her company. I wouldn't even like her going out for lunch with Ryder alone, and we all knew how deep he was in with Bailey. Still, if Indie was mine, I'd never give her up for anything. She would always come first.

She always did come first. Even now.

"Noted," I said with a nod and turned to see Indie wave at Jack. But he wasn't having any of that. He grabbed her and pulled her to his chest and slammed his mouth down on hers, leaning so far into the kiss that she had to arch backwards and grip his shoulders for support as he almost dipped her to the ground.

Over the top? Yes.

Unnecessary? Completely.

Was I jealous? More. Than. Anything.

Finally, after a long minute of being unable to look away from them making out like horny teenagers, Jack-ass got in the car and left.

"So, where to?" Indie smiled and skipped along beside me. She was a stark contrast to the person she was just minutes ago when Jack was still

72

around.

I unclenched my fists and relaxed my fingers. "Anywhere you like."

***

We ended up wandering around the small town and grabbing some street food, which I'd heard was amazing, and it did not disappoint. We walked the streets and checked out the market, then strolled along the white sand beach. I instantly wished I'd brought my board with me, so I could hit the crystal-clear waves. I was pretty sure the hotel had boards on the beach that guests could borrow, though there was nothing like surfing with your own board.

Before long, we'd moved away from the beach and into the rainforest. The canopy gave a much-needed reprieve from the heat of the sun.

"Oh, it's beautiful," Indie exclaimed, spreading her arms wide and tilting her head back.

"It is," I muttered, though I may have been directing my comment to her more than the rainforest.

"Can you hear that?" Her head snapped forward, and she tilted it to the side, listening carefully.

"Sounds like water." I nodded to my left where the sound of rushing water was coming from.

"Let's check it out." She grabbed my hand and dragged me down the narrow path, brushing aside leaves and overgrown branches as we went, until we came to a clearing that opened to a sparkling blue waterhole. Rocks and tropical plants surrounded it, and to the far right of the lake was a magnificent waterfall cascading over the edge of the cliff. Birds sang in the trees above us, sunlight filtered through the canopy above and reflected off the rippling water, tempting me to go for a swim.

It was serene.

Peaceful.

And totally secluded.

Not a soul in sight.

Indie slipped her shoes off and sat on a rock at the edge of the water. "Oh, it's cold," she cried, dipping her toes into the pool, her back to me. "Come feel the water, Linc."

I was going to feel the water, all right, but I was going for a swim instead. Peeling my shirt over my head, I kicked off my flip flops and dropped my shorts before gritting my teeth and running straight into the water. I must have startled Indie, because she shrieked as I darted past.

"Ahhh, freaking hell. It's cold." I dunked my head and swam a little way out, waiting for my body to adjust to the frigid temperature.

Indie's squeals had turned into laughter. "You're crazy!"

"The water's beautiful. You should come in." I swam a little closer to her, trying to hide my chattering teeth.

"You just finished screaming about how cold the water is. I'm not that stupid." She put her foot back in and kicked water at me.

One way or another, she was getting in that water.

I smiled at her. It wasn't a friendly smile. It was

sinister. Her eyes widened, and she moved back on the rock, knowing I was coming for her.

"You better lose that dress real quick, Princess. I'd hate for it to get wrecked." I crept closer. Panic marred her features. She knew all too well that I meant what I said.

"You wouldn't." She held her hands out to stop me.

"Come on. You know me better than that. You're getting in this water. It's just up to you whether your pretty dress is coming in with you." I turned my back to her. "You have until the count of three. If you're not in the water by then, I'm turning around regardless of whether you're still dressed or not."

"Linc, I'm not skinny-dipping with you." Her voice quivered a touch with nerves.

I chuckled. "No one said anything about skinny-dipping, but please don't let me stop you if you feel inclined to swim naked." I reached for the waistband of my boxers, and intending to mess with her a little more, I removed them completely. "I might just join you." I threw my underwear over my shoulder and onto the rock.

I was surely going to hell for this.

"Linc! Oh my God!" I looked over my shoulder at her to find her face buried in her hands.

"To the count of three, Indie," I warned one last time.

She huffed.

What was I doing? She was Nate's sister.

"One."

And she had Jack-ass for a boyfriend.

"Two."

She was completely off limits.

"Three."

It was silent. I turned to find her standing on the rock, twisting her hands nervously in front of her. Her dress…at her feet.

I gulped.

Lace. White lace. Matching.

Hell.

I was going to hell.

And I didn't care. I didn't care that she was Nate's sister. I didn't care that she had a boyfriend. I didn't care that she was entirely off limits. She was mine. Always had been. And one way or another, I wasn't leaving this island without getting what I wanted.

Forcing my eyes to remain on her face and not roam all over her smooth and creamy—there I went with the smooth and creamy thoughts again—exposed skin, I arched an eyebrow. "Well."

"I'm scared it's going to be cold."

"You'll get used to it," I promised.

"Okay." She smiled and took a step forward, but then she turned and climbed back over the rocks and darted off to the right. Where was she going?

"Indie," I shouted. "Where are you?"

She giggled. "You'll see."

"Dammit. Get back here. Don't go wandering off." I waded toward the shore and was climbing onto the rock where her yellow dress was when I heard it.

A wolf whistle.

I'd forgotten I was completely naked. Dropping

back in the water, I turned to see where the sound had come from.

And, sure enough, there was Indie at the top of the freaking cliff, right beside the waterfall.

"No. Don't you dare do it!" I yelled up to her, but it was useless. She wouldn't listen to me. It wasn't safe. There could be rocks. It could be shallow. There could be vines and branches she could get tangled up in. She could hit her head. Break her neck.

"Ready." She lifted her arms out to the side and screamed as she leapt forward over the edge of the cliff.

I couldn't watch her go down. My lifeguard instincts kicked in, so I dove and swam in the direction she would have hit the water, preparing for the worst. She had to be okay. She couldn't have hurt herself. She would be fine. Right? Panic was setting in. I'd seen something like this happen too many times. Guys being dared to jump into unknown water, getting caught in rips, seaweed, or misjudging the safe distance and smashing into the rocks. She had to be okay.

Coming up for a breath, I heard Indie before I saw her. "Oh my God, Linc. You're an idiot," she said, swimming for me.

I was the idiot? How? She just jumped off a damn cliff, and I was the idiot. She risked her life and scared me half to death, and I was the idiot.

"What the hell were you thinking, Indie?" I growled, coming to a stop right in front of her.

She pulled her arm back and punched me in the shoulder as I reached for her. "I didn't know where you went or what happened. I jumped, and you were gone." Her eyes were wide with fear, so I pulled her in close, my legs brushing hers as I treaded water to keep us both afloat. "I was scared," she sniffed into my shoulder.

"You—you were scared? Geez, Indie, I thought you hit shallow water, and...do you know how dangerous that was? Anything could have happened."

"I'm sorry, okay? I knew it was safe, though." She draped one arm around my neck, and the other rested on my shoulder.

"How?" I gulped, fully aware I was completely naked, and she was getting a little too close to be appropriate.

"There was a sign up the path from where I was sitting on the rock." She screwed her nose up in that cute way she did so often growing up to get out of trouble, and it worked. Every time.

How could I be mad at that face?

"Okay," I sighed.

Her fingers danced across my shoulder, circling the scar there, the only sign of the accident I'd had. Her lips pulled down into a frown. I expected her to say something about it, but she didn't. I didn't know why I expected a reaction, though. She hadn't seemed too concerned when it happened a year ago.

"Now we're here, so let's go for a swim." I released her, needing to put some distance between us.

We swam toward the waterfall, the torrent thundering down and churning around us the closer we got.

Indie dove first, swimming under the curtain of water raining down over the cliff, with me following close behind. We came up for air in the mouth of a small cave. The rush of the water was muted from the walls of rock around us.

"Wow," Indie breathed, looking back through the water into the clearing where we left our clothes. "It's beautiful."

"It is. Let's keep going." I swam slowly into the cave but stopped when I realised Indie wasn't following. "You coming or not?"

"Not. What if there are bats or something?"

"There are no bats, Princess."

"You don't know that."

"Trust me. I can see light up ahead. I think it opens at the top."

"Nope, you go. I'll stay here."

"Seriously. You'll jump off a cliff, but you won't swim twenty metres into a cave?"

"Well, I'm not stupid."

"I'm not going to win this, am I?"

"No. Have fun!" She waved her fingers at me, so I turned and swam away.

I wouldn't be long. I just wanted to see what was in there. And it turned out to be nothing. The hole in the top was barely a crack, and the light I saw was mostly reflection on the water. It was quite disappointing after the gorgeous waterfall and swimming hole. Deciding not to waste time, I dove under the water and headed straight back for Indie.

CHAPTER NINE

Indie

I hated treading water. The constant movement just to keep your head above. It was awful. My arms and legs were so tired, I gave up and swam to the rock walls and found a place I could grip onto while I waited. And waited.

I was thinking about swimming back out and getting dressed, because it was surely getting late, and we'd have to head back soon, when something brushed against my leg. I froze. *Ahhh.* What was that? It brushed my leg again, higher up this time, making me squirm. Did I stay still or swim away? It could have been a crocodile...Did they have them in Fiji? A piranha? Some sort of human-eating fish.

A shark. It was a shark, right? Seriously, it wasn't that much of a stretch. All the rivers on this island led back to the ocean at some point, didn't they? A shark could have easily swum upstream and...

Grabbed my thigh...

I held my breath because they smelled fear, or was that blood? A shark could have easily tickled my hips and made the water swirl around me. And a shark could just as easily have had blond dreadlocks.

"Dammit, Linc," I cried, letting go of the wall so I could shove his head underwater, which only made him laugh.

"Couldn't resist." He came up spluttering out a laugh and reached for the rock wall behind me, caging me in. "Sorry."

I had no choice but to hold onto his shoulders for support, or I'd drown. He was close. So close I could feel his body heat warming me through the chill in the water. Droplets clung to his eyelashes, dripped down his face and onto me. He was that close. What was he doing? His nose skimmed along my cheek, making my heart stutter. I was having palpitations. Oh God, I was going to have a heart attack, and all he did was wipe his nose on me. Gross!

If I turned my head the slightest bit, our lips would touch.

"Sorry isn't good enough. I thought you were a shark," I mumbled, leaning into him. Having him so close made my brain foggy.

"If I were a shark, I'd have done a hell of a lot more than run my hands over your legs." His lips grazed my ear as he spoke in that low, deep voice of his. Too afraid to trust my own voice completely, knowing it would quiver from nerves, I simply nodded. Lincoln Andrews was the only person who had the power to turn me into a nervous wreck.

With nothing more than a look or a few carefully chosen words, I was putty in his hands.

He brought one hand to the side of my face. I thought he was going to touch my cheek, brush away a stray hair, like the hero in all Bailey's romance novels did whenever he was face to face with the girl. But no, he pushed away from the wall and me, causing me to sink, and swiftly swam back out through the curtain of water falling overhead. Just like that, he was gone.

Taking a moment to catch my breath and slow my heartrate down, I swam after him. By the time I had made it back to my rock and my dress, he was fully clothed and scrolling through his phone.

I pulled myself onto the rocks and wrung my hair out so it would dry faster. Linc looked up at me and opened his mouth to say something but stopped. His eyes widened, and he bit his lip. His gaze made me uncomfortable. I shifted on my feet. What was wrong with him?

"What?" I asked, crossing my arms over my chest.

He twirled his hand in my direction, still not speaking.

"Spit it out, Linc."

He stood and took slow, deliberate steps until he stopped in front of me. His eyes focused on mine the entire time, and his hands clenched in fists at his sides. He was either going to punch me, which I knew was stupid because he'd never hurt me, or he was fighting with himself not to do something. I just didn't know what.

"Geez, Princess." His voice was gruff,

gravelly—he almost sounded sick as he dropped to his knees in front of me and rested one hand on my hip. My skin burned under his fingertips, and I may have stumbled forward, only catching myself when he reached up his other hand to stop me falling. My head was light and airy.

"You're killing me right now," he said, lazily dragging his eyes up to meet mine. One hand dropped from my hip, and he reached for the yellow fabric of my dress. "There's only so much I can take."

He released his hold and stood before me, my dress gripped in his white-knuckled fist. "Put this on before I do something that will get my ass kicked."

It was then I realised I was only wearing my white underwear. And...oh, no! White was see-through when wet. I took the dress from him without a word as he gave me one last lingering glance before turning and taking a few steps away.

Linc cleared his throat and spoke while I dressed hurriedly. "Kenzie is here with her friend Harper, and Brody has just arrived." He turned back to me with raised eyebrows.

"What?" I strapped up my sandal and stood, dusting off my dress and walking over to him.

"I didn't think Brody was coming," he said, guiding me over the last few rocks and onto the path.

Brody was my cousin and so much like Nate and Linc it was scary at times. He was the same age and used to hang around a lot growing up. He didn't get along with his parents. Well, no one got along with his parents. My father didn't even speak to his own brother anymore. They had some falling out years ago, but I never asked. I didn't want the details.

"I guess he was able to swing some time off at work." It was news to me as well, but it must have been hard. He recently graduated from paramedicine, and to be able to get a week off so soon after securing a long-term job must have been difficult.

"I guess. It'll be good to see him. And Kenzie brought a friend? What are you parents doing? Inviting the whole damn town?" Linc stepped over a log and ducked under some low-hanging branches, lifting them out of the way for me to walk through.

"Don't ask me. You seem to know more about their wedding than I do." I was struggling to keep up with him now. Was it this hard on the way in? Or were we going the wrong way?

"Not my fault you don't come home often enough," he shot back over his shoulder.

"It's entirely your fault," I mumbled to myself, not expecting him to hear me, but…

"What?" He turned so fast I lost my footing and stumbled backwards, catching myself on a tree before I hit the ground.

"Ouch," I hissed, turning my hand over to look at the gash running across my palm. There were small pieces of tree bark embedded in the skin, and blood was pouring out everywhere. My eyes crossed, my stomach churned, and then the earth began to tilt. Not even Linc's voice calling my name could pull me back.

***

I woke to Linc cursing in my ear. I opened my heavy eyelids and tried to stretch, only to have everything spin on its axis again. Linc cursed some more as my feet hit the ground.

"Careful, Princess," he said, keeping one arm around me while sliding the room key into his door. My head pounded, and my ears were ringing.

We were back at the hotel? And where was his shirt? Not that I was complaining.

"You passed out when you saw the blood." He kicked open the door and held me close as he led me inside. "Lie down."

Linc picked up the phone beside the bed and called the front desk for a first aid kit before walking into the bathroom, leaving me alone. Maybe Jack was right and Linc did have a saviour complex. But that was okay. I really didn't mind if it meant spending extra time with him.

I did what I was told, falling back into his pillows, and was disappointed they didn't smell like him. But they wouldn't, because he slept in my room last night, not here. It wasn't until I brought my hand up to brush my hair out of my face that I spotted Linc's shirt. Wrapped tightly around my palm.

He returned with a damp cloth and sat on the bed beside me. "It looks pretty nasty, but I think I can clean it up. You'll probably have to wear a bandage around it for a few days to keep it protected, though." He picked my hand up in his and gently unwrapped his shirt. "I'm so sorry, Indie. I didn't mean for you to get hurt."

"It wasn't your fault. I fell. I'm clumsy, remember?" I smiled and watched his face, refusing to look at my hand because I'd likely pass out again. And besides, Linc's face was a much nicer view.

He chuckled. "I remember."

He came to my rescue all the time growing up because I was always injuring myself or someone else. We were playing football once, and I was running up the field with the ball, trying to get closer to where Linc was so I could kick it to him. Brody came from nowhere and tackled me to the ground. In my efforts to get him off me, I twisted and turned and kicked every way I could, until I finally landed one kick on him, right between his legs. It wouldn't have been so bad if Nate hadn't taken that moment to lean over us and try to rip the ball from my hands, though. Brody reared back in pain and consequently smashed the back of his head into Nate's face.

Brody ended up with a cracker of a headache and bruised groin. Nate walked away with a broken nose. And I...I was carried off the field in the arms of a laughing Linc because I managed to sprain my knee during the whole ordeal. I was never allowed to play football with them again.

There was a knock at the door, so Linc stood to answer it, returning moments later with a small white case adorned with a drawn-on red cross. I guessed that was the first aid kit.

"Hopefully, this has something we can use." He twisted his mouth in doubt.

I lay perfectly still, not wanting to risk a glance at my hand for fear of throwing up. Instead, I continued to watch Linc. The way his tongue darted out and wet his lips in concentration. The blue flecks in his grey eyes. The scruffy stubble across his jaw that I really wanted to touch. I could watch him for hours and never get bored.

"There. All done." He placed my hand on my stomach and turned to pack up the medical kit.

"Was it bad?" I asked, not really wanting to know the answer.

"No, just a scratch. It'll be fine."

"Thank you."

"If you're feeling up to it, Ryder called before because Bailey couldn't get hold of you. She wants to have a girls' night."

If I wasn't mistaken, a frown crossed his features before he schooled them into something more relaxed.

"Oh, umm...I guess. What are you doing?" I cringed the second I asked. I didn't want to sound desperate or clingy, but the truth was, I was desperate and clingy. I didn't want to leave this room. I wanted to spend more time in his company. I saw Bailey all the time. Kenzie, not so much, but...Linc, I never saw him anymore.

"Nate says we're going to the bar downstairs for a few games of pool. All of us. Him, Brody, Ryder, and me."

"What about Jack?" I watched as Linc's eyebrows screwed up.

"Yeah, him too." He walked over to his closet and began rummaging through his clothes. "You should probably go and get ready too. It's dinner. You might want to charge your phone and call Bailey," he said, talking to me like I was a child. What was his problem? He walked into his bathroom and closed the door, effectively dismissing me.

I was gone by the time he got out of the shower.

CHAPTER TEN

Linc

The music was blaring, and my clothes stuck to my body. The smell of sweat lingered in the air, but the guys all seemed to be having a good time playing pool and drinking beer. I wasn't in the mood. One thing had been running through my head all day. Okay, that was a lie. Two things had been running through my head all afternoon.

Indie…Indie swimming in her white lace underwear. Indie standing on that rock dripping wet while she tried to dry her hair, only to have the water run down her body, trickling over her curves, glistening in the sun. That was the single most sexy thing I had ever seen. I'd never get that image out of my head. I never wanted to get that image out of my head. In fact, I was keeping it. It was going in the spank bank for later reference.

And then I couldn't stop thinking about the comment she made before she fell into the tree and fainted. My fault. I heard it clear as day. It was my fault she didn't come home anymore, and I couldn't figure out why. I didn't think I'd ever given her a reason not to come home, so why was she avoiding it? Or avoiding me? My mind ran through a million scenarios and came up empty every time.

"What's got you looking like you're in pain?" Brody put a beer on the table in front of me, snapping me out of my thoughts.

"Where is everyone?" I looked up and noticed the pool table was empty.

"Gone to the nightclub up the street. That Ryder dude really doesn't like his girl being away from him for too long, does he? He got trust issues or what?"

"Nah, not at all, not with Bailey, at least. Protective, though. He doesn't trust other blokes."

"I can see why. She's hot."

"Not my type." Best mates' younger sisters were more my type, unfortunately. I took a swig of my beer and asked the obvious. "Are the girls at the club?"

"Yeah, apparently. So Jack and Nate wanted to get over there too and keep an eye on Indie. Told 'em we'd be there after this drink." He tipped his beer to his mouth. "So what's got you looking all torn up?"

"Nothing. I'm fine."

"Bull. Three guesses. Indie." He counted on one finger. "Jack." Two fingers. "And...hmm, Indie." Three fingers with a smirk.

"Don't know what you're talking about." I turned to the side to watch the action in the bar, not that it was interesting, but it was better than looking at Brody's piercing gaze.

"You took too long, man." He leaned across the table and punched me in the shoulder. "You missed your chance."

I didn't say anything. He didn't know what he was talking about. He couldn't know. I'd never told anyone how I felt about her, particularly not Brody or Nate. They were family. They'd kill me.

"Fine. Don't admit it to me. Just know I think you're an idiot for blowing it." He drained the rest of his beer and slapped his hand on the table. "Let's go."

***

The nightclub wasn't much better than the bar. Too hot and too many people bumping and grinding against each other. I didn't see the appeal of places like this at all. They were sleazy, dirty, and full of losers trying to prey on young, hot women, like Indie. Bailey. Kenzie. Harper. I gritted my teeth and shoved my hands in my pockets as I edged my way toward the bar.

"Whiskey." I nodded to the bartender because beer just wouldn't cut it tonight.

"On the hard stuff now, huh?" Brody shouted in my ear after ordering himself a beer.

I slumped against the bar. I was on the hard stuff now, only because it made dealing with Jack-ass a little easier. "Where is everyone?"

He tilted his beer bottle toward the centre of the dance floor, where I could just make out Kenzie's mass of blonde curls and Nate's terrible dance moves. "Come on. Don't be a stick in the mud." He nudged me with his elbow.

I wasn't a stick in the mud. I just didn't want to go over there and dance when I had a perfectly good spot at the bar with a regular supply of liquor.

"I'm fine here. You go. You look like you're itching to bust out some moves."

"Your loss, man. Indie's there." He slapped me on the back and walked off, leaving me to nurse my whiskey.

Everyone greeted him when he made it to their little circle, which had now shifted closer to the edge of the floor. Indie stood on her toes and wrapped her arms around him in a hug and proceeded to hang off his shoulder until Jack-ass finally pulled her away.

They danced together. Like couples did. But they were too close. Their hips were touching too often. His hands were everywhere. In places they shouldn't have been. Her hands were holding onto him. Touching his neck. His hair.

My eyebrows pinched together, and my jaw hurt from clenching it so hard. I was considering getting up and leaving when I noticed Jack-ass dragging her toward the door while she struggled to get out of his hold. I stood at once and moved in their direction.

"Jack, stop. I don't want to go," Indie tried to argue with him as I reached her side.

"Don't care, Indie. What the hell were you thinking, huh? Wearing something like that to a nightclub," he hissed at her. "You look like a whore."

She stopped dead in her tracks, causing him to

jerk backwards.

I grabbed Indie by the arm and put her behind me. Squaring my shoulders, I glared at Jack. "That was out of line. Apologise."

"Whatever. Look at her. Every single guy in this club can't take his eyes off her." Jack looked around the club, my gaze following his, and I realised he was right. Not everyone, but a lot of guys were looking at her because she looked gorgeous.

"Still no need to speak to her that way."

"Look, bro, I don't care right now. I'm done. I'm tired. She can either come back to the hotel with me like the good little girlfriend she is, or she can stay here, and you can deal with her."

I turned to face her. "What do you want to do, Princess?"

"Stay," she breathed hesitantly, her gaze darting over my shoulder at Jack. Was she scared of him?

"Fine. Don't come knocking on my door in the middle of the night, baby cakes. I won't answer." And with that, he turned and stormed out.

"You okay?" I asked.

"Fine."

"Want to go back over and dance?"

"No, I need a drink."

"I can help with that." I grabbed her hand and pulled her toward the bar.

Two tequila slammers later, she had me on the dance floor with everyone else. Somehow, Nate ended up dancing with Harper, and Brody was wrapped around Kenzie, completely oblivious to the threatening glares Ryder was sending his way. I kept my distance, dancing beside Indie.

93

That was until some loser worked his way into the middle of our small group and began grinding against Indie. She looked at me with wide eyes and tried to step away, but he wrapped his arm around her waist and pulled her against him. I took one step forward and crossed my arms.

"Back off, man. We're just having fun," he said with a sneer. The gel in his hair made it stick straight up like a porcupine.

"Does it look like she's having fun?" I asked, aware Nate, Brody, and Ryder were watching closely.

"I don't hear her complaining." She was struggling against his hold.

"Well, I am. Piss off and leave my girl alone." I grabbed Indie's hands and pulled her against me, where she fit perfectly.

"Sorry, man. My bad." He held his hands up in surrender before scurrying away after one look at Nate and Brody flanking me on either side.

Indie waited until the douche with too much gel had disappeared before trying to move away from me.

"Uh-uh." I pulled her so her back was pressed to my chest. "You're staying right here with me."

I expected an argument or for her to roll her eyes at me and tell me I was being an idiot, but she didn't. No, she relaxed into me and began dancing, swinging her hips to the beat of the music, one hand raised in the air, the other gripping my forearm tightly to her waist, which was perfectly okay with me. I hated dancing, but that was how much I loved that girl.

We moved together languidly. I had no idea if we were keeping time to the music or not, and I didn't care. I was just enjoying the moment while it lasted. No way would Nate be okay with me dancing with his sister like I was if it hadn't been for the other loser trying to get under her dress. I didn't know how long we danced, but it was long enough that the others had stopped for a breather and a drink or two. Yet we continued dancing, only stopping when Kenzie came running over to tell us, "Body shots!"

"Body shots?" Indie looked at me with a quirked eyebrow. "You game?"

I gulped. Hell yes, I was game, but I didn't want to face the repercussions. Nate would kill me in my sleep if I so much as glanced at the wrong body part, let alone did shots.

"You have to. It'll be fun." Indie laughed as she pulled me over to the table where there were sixteen shot glasses filled with what I assumed was tequila since there was a salt shaker and a bowl of sliced lemon.

"All right! Let's do this!" Nate cheered. His eyes were glassy, a red tinge covered his cheeks, and he swayed a little on his feet.

"How much has he had to drink?" Indie asked.

"No idea." I held her in front of me as we watched Nate pull his shirt off. What the hell was he doing?

"Okay, Harper, when you're ready." He winked. I rolled my eyes, Indie groaned, and Harper giggled. Jesus.

Body shots were incredibly uncomfortable to

watch. All the licking, drinking, sucking. It was gross. At least until it was my turn to taste Indie's skin. Everyone else had taken their shots. Nate and Harper, Brody and Kenzie—much to Ryder's disgust—Ryder and Bailey, and now it was our turn. I was just hoping Nate had had enough to drink that he didn't care I was about to lick his sister and suck a lemon wedge out of her mouth.

Damn. Dreams really did come true.

I stepped back to examine Indie in her tight, strapless silver dress, trying to decide where I wanted to put the salt, but she had other ideas.

"Shirt, please?" she asked, holding out her hand to me.

I looked down. I was not taking my shirt off. "No."

"Come on, man. Don't be a wimp." This from Nate.

I rubbed my hand over my face. Fine. They asked for it. I pulled my t-shirt over my head and handed it to Indie.

"Hmm…" She tapped her finger to her lips in contemplation. I didn't like being studied that way, but I couldn't deny I liked her looking at me all the same.

She twirled her finger, indicating for me to turn around.

"Perfect." Her voice was soft as her hand wrapped around me from behind, bringing a lemon wedge to my lips. "Okay, you ready?"

I nodded, my back still to her. Her fingers danced along my back for a moment, but then the warmth of her breath caressed my shoulder blades, just before her tongue slid across my spine, directly in the centre of my shoulders. A few seconds passed, and I knew she was sprinkling the salt over the place she licked. Her fingers pressed into my biceps, and her tongue darted out and swiped across my spine. Not once. Not twice. But three times, licking up every granule of salt from my overheating skin. A groan escaped my lips, and my eyes might have rolled into the back of my head. Why did that feel so good? Turning, I caught her just as she swallowed down her shot before standing on the tips of her toes to lean in close and bite into the lemon that was still hanging from my lips. It took every ounce of self-control I could muster not to drop that lemon and kiss her senseless.

Dammit. I should have gone first. How was I supposed to do a body shot when all I wanted to do was run my tongue over every square inch of her skin?

"Your turn." Indie smiled and handed me the salt shaker then put another lemon wedge in her mouth. I licked my lips, suddenly feeling parched.

Reaching over the table, I plucked an ice cube from the wine bucket and turned to smile at Indie. Her eyes widened, and she stood perfectly still. Brushing her hair over her left shoulder, I traced below her collarbone with my finger, watching as her chest rose and fell rapidly, before following the same line with the ice cube. I dragged the frozen block of water across her warm skin and watched goose bumps appear on her flesh.

I popped the ice cube into my mouth and sprinkled the salt shaker over her collarbone.

Reaching for my shot, I chanced a glance at Nate, but he was too engrossed in a conversation with Harper to notice what I was doing. Brody gave me a knowing look. Ryder appeared to be bored, and Bailey sat, watching with rapt attention, which I found a little weird but brushed aside.

"Ready?"

"Uh-huh." Her voiced sounded choked, strangled, like she could barely speak.

I dipped my head, taking advantage of the fact that Nate seemed to have been swept off his feet by Harper, and gently dragged my nose down the column of Indie's throat before sliding my tongue across her skin, swirling and licking all the salt clean, sucking slightly on the protruding bone. Why? Because I wanted to drive her as crazy as she drove me. I felt her gasp rather than heard it, and that was enough for me to know it was working. Pulling back, I downed the shot and didn't hesitate to wrap my lips around the lemon wedge between her teeth. Our mouths brushed as I sucked on the fruit, getting every drop of juice I could. I didn't know who dropped the lemon first, but it fell to the floor at our feet while I traced my tongue along her lips, lapping up the tartness left over from the citrus fruit.

Indie's legs gave out. Wrapping my arms around her, I caught her just before she fell.

Brody cleared his throat. Kenzie studied me curiously with the exact same look her brother was giving me.

"That was, umm…interesting." Bailey laughed. "I felt like I was intruding on an intimate moment."

"Nothing intimate about body shots," I lied. That body shot was undeniably intimate, but I didn't want to call attention to it, not when Nate hadn't noticed, but everyone else appeared to have.

"Umm...Well, I'm tired. So I'm gonna head back. Night, guys," Indie announced, wrapping her arms around her chest and turning away from me. She waved to everyone and walked toward the door, leaving me staring after her like a complete fool.

"You're an idiot," Bailey and Brody said the same time, looking at me like I had just told them I was a blue alien from Mars.

"What did I do?" I really didn't know. She said she was tired, but she could have at least waited thirty seconds for me.

"Go," Ryder and Kenzie ordered simultaneously. Like some freaky twin thing, they ushered me away from the table and after Indie.

CHAPTER ELEVEN

Indie

He was such a jerk. Completely clueless. I shouldn't have let his comment bother me, because I should have been used to it by now, but I did. It hurt. I wouldn't do body shots with just anyone. I couldn't even date anyone because I always compared them to him, and then he went and brushed it off like it was nothing.

"Indie, wait!" he called from behind me. I didn't stop or turn around. I only wanted to go back to the hotel.

"Hey." He fell into step beside me. "You can't walk back by yourself."

I ignored him and kept walking. I wasn't wasting any more time on him. I really wasn't. We continued silently side by side until I stumbled on the cracks in the concrete path. Linc's hand shot out and grabbed my elbow, steadying me.

"Sorry," I mumbled. Stupid heels and tequila didn't mix. Me and heels in general didn't mix.

"What was everyone else doing?" I was making small talk because the silence felt weird, uncomfortable.

"Drinking. I think they're all going to be very sick tomorrow. Probably won't even leave their rooms."

Wc were approaching another bar with a loud group of—I squinted to see better—men and their motorbikes out the front. A biker bar in Fiji?

"I wish you weren't wearing that dress right now." Linc tensed beside me.

"Excuse me?" Was he telling me I looked like a whore as well? It was not my fault. It was all Jack and Bailey's stupid idea to replace my clothes and make me dress like...this.

"You think I look like a whore too?" I stopped walking, a frown tugging at my lips.

"No, of course not." He stopped and faced me, his left hand coming to rest on my hip, while his right traced the neckline of my low-cut dress. My breath hitched. "I love this dress on you. But—"

"But?" There was always a but.

"You're going to attract all the wrong attention, like back in the club."

I cringed at the thought of the greasy guy who tried to dance with me. He smelled of stale beer and onions. I wanted to throw up. Yuck.

Linc dropped his hands and shifted me to his other side, putting himself between me and where the bikers were already whistling and calling out.

Slinging his arm over my shoulder, he pulled me against him. With my head tucked under his chin, he directed us across the street away from the bar, keeping me shielded from the leering creepers hanging out on the footpath. Once we were a safe distance from the bar and the street was quiet, I expected Linc to drop his arm and let me go, but he didn't. He kept me close until we reached the door to his room.

"Well, goodnight. Thanks for walking me back." I stepped over to my door, but then I froze. "Dammit."

"What's wrong?"

"My room key. Jack has it." I pinched the bridge of my nose, already feeling a headache forming. I would bet that was his plan. Leave me alone at the club and take my room key so I had no choice but to call him or go to Linc's room. He'd expect me to do the latter, but I had news for him. I was going to call him, wake him up, and make him bring me my key. It was only—I checked my thin silver watch—four a.m. It was only fair after calling me a whore when he knew damn well I wasn't.

I didn't have my phone. Jack had it. I groaned and dropped my head to the door, banging it a few times. Why did Jack like to torture me? It was like he was doing everything in his power to force me and Linc together, but it wouldn't work. Lincoln didn't see me that way. I was like his little sister. He'd made that perfectly clear on many occasions, and I was stupid for holding out hope. Jack was only making it worse.

"What's wrong?" Linc touched my shoulder.

I pulled my head back to look at him. "Jack has my phone, too."

"Why?" He stepped away and nodded at his

102

door, indicating for me to follow him.

So I'd do exactly this. Follow him into his room for the night.

"In his pockets, so I didn't have to carry everything all night."

"Here," he pulled his phone out and handed it to me, "call him."

I smiled gratefully and took the phone, punching in Jack's number quickly and putting it to my ear. It rang three times before he answered.

"Tell me you're in his room right now."

"Yes," I sighed.

"So why are you calling me at four a.m.?"

"Because—"

"You want me to join you?" He cackled into the phone, sounding far too excited by the thought.

"No! I need my room key."

"Nope, sorry. You're just going to have to stay with lover boy."

"Please, Jack. Please bring it up for me," I begged, my voice catching at the end. I'd had too much to drink, and I was still hurt from Linc's comments earlier. For some reason, my head kept replaying every conversation and interaction we'd ever had that turned bad, that usually ended with me crying myself to sleep. From our first kiss in my dad's office, to the time I thought he was going to kiss me again when I returned home for the summer holidays after being away for most of the year, only to jump back in shock and mutter something about "little sister," and to every other time he acted like he cared, flirted, looked after me, only to ruin it by dismissing it as nothing.

But it was never nothing. Not to me.

"Okay, baby cakes, I'll be right there." Jack's voice softened in understanding.

"Thanks." I hung up and handed the phone back to Linc, who was pacing the room, pulling on his hair.

"So?"

"Jack's on his way up." I stood and moved toward the door, intending to wait outside.

"Stay. Wait here for him," Linc said. "I'll get you a water."

"Water?" I turned and crossed my arms, watching him curiously. He pulled a bottle of water from the mini fridge and gave it to me.

"You've had a lot to drink. You should drink all of that before you go to bed. Have you got painkillers for the morning?"

So we were back to the caring big brother act. And this was why my head was always a mess around him. I didn't know which way was up. "I think so."

We stood awkwardly facing each other, me taking sips of my water, unscrewing the lid, and putting it back on, over and over. Finally, after what felt like hours but was more like two minutes, the door burst open and Jack came charging in.

"I'm so sorry, baby cakes. I was a jerk before." He cupped my face with his hands, weaving his fingers through my hair and tilting my face up to his. What was he doing now? "Forgive me."

"Of cour—" I didn't even finish speaking before Jack's mouth came down on mine, hard, dominating, intense. *Whoa*. Who knew he could kiss like that? My knees actually buckled, and I had to cling to him to stop from falling. He smiled. The jerk smiled into the kiss, knowing he knocked me off my feet. His hands travelled down my back, pausing on my butt to give it a squeeze.

He broke the kiss and looked over my shoulder at Linc. "Thanks for looking after her tonight. I owe you, man." He held out his fist to bump with Linc's. Then Jack did the one thing I least expected. He gripped my legs and lifted me up, forcing my ankles to lock behind his back so I didn't fall. Oh my God. It was awful. Horrifying. So awkward and inappropriate. "But, ahhh...we should get going now," he said, giving my ass a light slap.

He slapped me.

He was a dead man.

I couldn't look even look at Linc. I was so embarrassed. Instead, I buried my face in Jack's shoulder and wished the ground would open and swallow me whole.

He carried me to my room, not releasing me until we were at my bed, where he promptly dropped me on top like a hot potato before throwing himself down beside me.

I sat up and straightened my dress, which had ridden so scandalously high it would even make Her Royal Whoreness Christina blush, and that was saying a lot. Christina was a hussy, to put it mildly. She was sleeping with Bailey's ex-boyfriend when he and Bailey were still together in high school. And to make things worse, she and Bailey were best friends at the time. Couldn't get more skanky than that.

"What was that?" I seethed at Jack.

"That," he paused for dramatic effect, "was a lot of fun."

My lips pinched, and my eyebrows joined. "That was embarrassing, and unnecessary, and—"

"Fun. Admit it. You liked kissing me. I made your knees wobble." He laughed and threw himself onto the pillow Linc had slept on the previous night.

My eyes widened, and I lurched forward, ripping the pillow out from under him. "Not that one," I clarified when he looked at me like I'd lost my mind. Maybe I had. But it still smelled like him. I might even pack it in my bag when I left here.

"Okaaaay...crazy pants." He sat up. "Now, where were we? Oh, yeah!" He snapped his fingers and grinned at me. "Wobbly knees and passionate kisses."

I shook my head and thought of something to change the subject. "So what did you do today?"

"Nuh-uh. We were talking about us." He flicked his hand between us.

"There is no us, Jack."

"I'm hurt, baby cakes. Real bad. Right here." A pained expression crossed his face as he beat his chest over his heart twice with his fist. Idiot.

"You'll live." I rolled my eyes and climbed off the bed to grab my pyjamas.

"Not if I don't get to experience more of your kisses." He was smooth. Sometimes.

"Do you sweet talk all your girlfriends?" I laughed because he didn't have girlfriends or boyfriends. He was committed to playing the field.

"Only you, sweet cheeks," he called out when I

106

closed the bathroom door behind me so I could dress for bed in peace.

I pulled on the tiny pink "Kiss My..." top and decided to slide Linc's black basketball shorts on instead because they were much more comfortable than the booty shorts Jack had bought. And besides, they were Linc's.

I returned to the room, and Jack stared, slack-jawed. "The top looks great. But those are not the shorts to match."

"I know. I wouldn't call that scrap of matching material shorts. They were tiny, Jack!"

"So...where did these abnormally large shorts come from?"

"Linc," I huffed, making Jack laugh again.

"Yes! It's working." He clapped his hands.

"It's not."

"You should have seen his face after I kissed you. He was insanely jealous. Did he dance with you tonight at the club? He did, didn't he? I bet he did. He would have been all macho and charged onto the dance floor like..." Jack stood and flexed his biceps, pulling his face into a frown. "Back off, creepy dude. She's mine."

I pressed my lips together to stifle the laugh that was threatening to escape, but I couldn't. He wasn't far off.

"I knew it! Lincoln 'I should have been a Greek God' Andrews saves the damsel again." Jack threw himself back on the bed and patted the space next to him. I curled up beside him, my eyelids getting heavy.

"I don't know, Jack. He's hot and cold. I think

this whole plan of yours might be useless."

"It's not useless. Trust me. This will work. He wants you. I know it. He just doesn't want to admit it because you're Nate's sister. But no matter what, he can't stay away from you."

"I hope you're right."

"I am." He wrapped his arm around my shoulder and pressed a kiss to my head. "We are going to get you your man, one way or another."

I smiled into his chest. I was grateful to have him as a friend. He'd do just about anything for me.

"You're not a bad kisser, you know, baby cakes," Jack murmured after a few minutes of silence.

"What?"

"Not bad. I mean, the earth didn't move, and you didn't make my knees shake, like I so clearly did you, but overall, it wasn't bad."

"Not bad?"

"I'd give it a solid C."

"A C? You're grading my kiss?" I sat up and punched him in the shoulder. "A kiss, mind you, that I didn't even want or expect. Are you forgetting one thing?"

"What?" he hissed, rubbing his palm over the spot I hit him. Good. Served him right.

"That I have only ever kissed two people. You…and him." I pointed at the door separating my room and Linc's.

"Well, do you want to practice? I'd be more than willing to sacrifice myself, to make sure you sweep the sexy lifeguard off his feet. Take one for the team and all."

"No! I don't want to practice!"

"Are you sure?" Jack wiggled his eyebrows.

"Yes," I breathed. At least I didn't think I wanted to practice. Did I? *Urgh*, I was confused. I'd never given any thought to the fact that I hadn't kissed anyone since Linc on my eighteenth birthday and that I was terrible at it. I was so inexperienced. I should practice so when Linc finally realised...

No, that was stupid. It wasn't going to happen, so what did it matter that I wasn't an expert kisser?

"Well, the offer is there if you need."

"I need to go to sleep. That's what I need."

"Okay, I'll see you tomorrow. Night, baby cakes." Jack rolled over, grabbed my face in his hands, and kissed me. On the mouth. Again. "Sorry, couldn't resist." He chuckled then pulled away and walked to the door.

"Idiot." I threw a pillow at his head but missed because he darted out of the room and closed the door behind him.

Reluctantly, I got up from the bed to get the pillow and lie back down when the door handle between the two rooms jiggled.

I went over and opened it a crack.

"Hey." Linc peered around the door. "Why was the door locked?"

"Hi. Must've been the staff," I lied and returned to my bed. I pulled back the covers and climbed in. What was he doing here? It had to be close to five a.m.

"Just wanted to check you were okay. I heard you shout and the door close. Where's Jack?" He stepped into the room and looked around.

"He left. I'm fine. Just tired." I snuggled into my pillow, which wasn't nearly as comfortable as sleeping on Linc's chest, but I made use of what I had. It smelled like him, so I wasn't complaining too much.

"Okay. Well, goodnight," he said softly, smoothing his hands over his hair.

"Night." I yawned, closing my eyes.

The bed dipped beside me, jolting me from the brink of sleep only moments later.

"Sorry, just wanted to make sure you had water and painkillers for when you woke up." I thought I smiled, or at least I tried to, but I was so tired, my eyes drooped closed again. "I'll go now. Everything is on your side table."

"Stay," I mumbled into the pillow and reached for his hand, or arm, or leg. Anything I could grab to stop him from leaving.

"Okay."

CHAPTER TWELVE

Linc

Nate rang me in the morning, waking me from a restless sleep, to tell me we were playing golf with his dad later. I'd tossed and turned all night. Having Indie sleep beside me made things so much worse. I couldn't shut my brain off. I needed to figure things out. I either had to make a move, bite the bullet, and tell Indie how I felt, or I had to learn to leave well enough alone. I was of two minds, constantly warring with myself, and it was driving me crazy.

On one hand, I didn't want to ruin my friendship with Nate. Something I knew without a doubt would happen if I told him I was in love with his sister. There would be no way he'd let me live to see another day. He tied Timmy Fullson, the scrawny kid who lived on the other side of him, to the light pole down the street because he called Indie pretty. And we were friends with that kid at the time.

And besides, he knew exactly what I was like.

111

I'd not had a long-term girlfriend except for the mistake that was Jasmine. What could I say? The body glitter and nipple tassels were intriguing for three seconds when my brain short circuited and I tried to push Indie out of my mind, but I couldn't marry a stripper. So there was no chance he'd let me date his sister.

And then…what if after all that, Indie didn't feel the same way? What if she laughed in my face and called me a loser? I'd have lost both her and Nate, and I didn't want to do that. They were too important to me.

But on the other hand, if Indie felt the same way and loved me as much as I did her, the risk of losing Nate as a friend, and my manhood in the process, would be totally worth it, right? If I had her by my side, nothing else mattered.

I was doomed if I did and doomed if I didn't.

***

The sun was scorching. I could feel my skin burning. My throat was dry, parched. A cold glass of water or eight wouldn't go astray. The golf game was taking forever, mostly because none of us was up for it, except Jack and Ryder. Ryder didn't look like he'd spent the entire night drinking in a club like the rest of us. He had a little black around the eyes, but that was it. Nate's face was pasty white, and he was sweating profusely and groaned every time he breathed. I was pretty sure Brody had thrown up after every hole, and Jack was his chipper old self. He wasn't tired at all, or sick. And he was hitting better than everyone else, including Steve, who was mildly impressed. What I wouldn't give to know exactly what he thought of his daughter's boyfriend.

"So what happened last night?" Brody asked, coming to stand beside me. He rested one arm on my shoulder for support because I was pretty sure he'd collapse otherwise.

"You were there. A lot of alcohol." I watched Nate take a swing at the golf ball on the eighteenth hole and miss, silently grateful the game was almost over.

"After you left with Indie." He groaned and crouched down, holding his stomach.

"Nothing. I walked her back to the hotel, and she went to bed." I dug the club into the ground, acting like last night was no big deal. I couldn't tell him I spent the night with her because she asked me to, because that would be stupid. I might as well shoot myself in the foot. But it was a big deal.

I hadn't planned on staying in her room. I just wanted to give her the water and painkillers to make sure she woke up okay. I intended to leave the door open between our rooms, just in case. I didn't like it when she drank so much, but she asked me to stay, and who was I to say no? I didn't the first time she got drunk and asked me to stay, back when she was in high school.

She'd gone to a party at that douche Chace's house—the one who knocked up Ryder's sister and cheated on Bailey—and drank too much. I blamed Jayden, Ryder's friend, for it, whether it was his fault or not. I didn't know. But she was with him and had too many cocktails, but then he left her there. Alone. When she called me at one a.m. to come get her, I was ready to beat someone up. Unfortunately, there was no one around who deserved it. Ryder had already taken care of Chace. So I found Indie locked in a room by herself—at least she'd had the sense to get away from everyone else—and took her home. I knew Steve and Leanne would have hit the roof had I brought her home drunk, so I took her back to my place, put her in my bed, and was planning to let her sleep it off alone, until she asked me to stay. I was weak. I couldn't say no to anything that girl asked, so I climbed into my bed beside her and held her all night.

"Fine, keep your secrets, but it's all going to come out eventually, man. You can't keep something like that bottled up for too long and not explode." He pulled himself to his feet and took his shot rather slowly.

"What do you mean?" Brody was way more perceptive than I gave him credit for.

"Tell her how you feel."

"Who? What?" I acted dumb, trying to pretend I didn't understand what he was talking about, but I knew it was useless. He knew. Somehow, he knew.

"Indie. Tell her how you feel. What's the worst that could happen?"

"Uh, Nate would murder me." I sighed. It felt good to finally admit it to someone.

"Nate wouldn't hurt a fly, and you know it."

"Maybe, but he'd definitely kick my ass and never speak to me again."

"No, he wouldn't," Brody argued, stopping short

when Ryder came over.

"How're you travelling, man?" Ryder laughed and slapped him on the back.

"Fine, just telling idiot here to 'fess up to Indie." Dammit.

"Will you shut up?" I shoved him in the chest.

"What? It's not like he doesn't know." Brody laughed. I looked at Ryder, and he nodded.

"Really?"

"Kind of hard not to figure it out," Ryder said and walked off again.

It wasn't that obvious, was it?

Brody chuckled.

It was that obvious.

"Linc, your shot," Nate called out.

I teed up the ball and took a swing. It soared through the air perfectly, landing on the green at the other end. I wasn't half bad at golf when I was in the mood to play.

"Nice," Nate cheered, getting a little life back in him.

The rest of the game went quickly, for which I was grateful. And then Steve announced he was buying us all drinks at the bar. Nate and Brody groaned. Ryder looked at his watch like he had somewhere better to be, and I was willing to bet that was wherever Bailey was. It didn't worry me what we did. I could do with a drink. Or a sleep. If things kept going the way they were this week, I was going to end up an insomniac with a drinking problem.

"So, last night?" Nate fell into step beside me as we followed his old man back to the bar. My stomach dropped. He didn't know, did he? He couldn't.

"Mmmm," I muttered.

"Harper," he said.

I closed my eyes and smiled. He didn't know. "What about her?"

"She's fun, right? Seems like a pretty cool chick."

"Yeah, I guess so. Why?"

"I don't know," he said then went silent.

"What happened after I left?"

"A lot of alcohol, man. Too much. I don't really remember, but when I woke up this morning, I wasn't alone." He ran his hands over his face and groaned. "And I don't remember it."

"So, Harper?"

"Harper." He nodded as we walked in the door to the restaurant.

"Nice." I laughed at his confused expression.

"You boys want to eat?" Steve asked.

"Yes!" everyone shouted in his face.

"Okay then, table for six. Thanks." He smiled at the waitress and followed her to a booth in the back.

Steve ordered us a round of beer, and even though we'd all had a pretty big night—some more than others, judging by Nate's and Brody's appearances today—the beers went down well, quenching our thirst from playing eighteen holes in the blistering heat.

And food had never tasted so good. I hadn't realised how hungry I was until my meal arrived. Everyone devoured everything on their plate.

"Big night?" Steve chuckled.

"Could say that," Nate mumbled through a mouthful of food.

"Well, you boys remember, tomorrow night is the rehearsal dinner, so you need to be sober. I don't want any hangovers for my wedding the following day."

"Whatever. It's not like it's your first wedding. And besides, you're remarrying Mum, so it doesn't have to be perfect."

"It does. This is what your mother wants, so it will be perfect. We never got a real wedding the first time, so this is it." Steve wiped his mouth with his napkin and set it on his plate.

"What do you mean, you didn't get a real wedding the first time?" Nate asked.

"Just that we got married at city hall in front of two random witnesses we met on the street. That's why this wedding is such a big deal. So, please, stay sober tomorrow night."

"Sure." I nodded. I didn't want to drink anymore, anyway.

"Okay," Nate agreed, followed by the rest.

"Good. Now, I'm off for my suit fitting. You boys stay here and enjoy ringing everything up on my bill." Steve stood and clapped Nate on the shoulder. "Oh, and before I forget, Nate. You and Lincoln need to be in the ballroom upstairs in the hotel at four p.m. for a dance lesson." He smiled and walked out.

"Why?" Nate groaned and banged his head on the table. So much like Indie. "Why? Why? Why? I hate dancing."

"It's one dance. Get over it," Ryder said.

117

"I can give you some pointers if you like," Jack offered. He'd been so quiet, I'd almost forgotten he was there.

"No. Thanks." Nate scowled and signalled the bartender for another round of beers.

It was going to be a long afternoon.

CHAPTER THIRTEEN

Indie

The bed was empty when I woke up again. This time I wasn't surprised, partly because I slept until after noon and only woke up when Bailey banged on the door.

"Why are you still asleep?" she asked, barging past me.

"Because I'm tired." I slumped against the door, hoping she'd get the hint and leave. She didn't.

"Well, get in the shower, wake yourself up, and get dressed. We're going out for lunch." She smiled and grabbed my shoulders, pushing me toward the bathroom. She was far too chipper considering how late we were out last night.

After my shower, I returned to my room to find Bailey had laid out my clothes on the bed like I was child. "I can pick my own clothes, you know?"

"Just saving time," she said as I picked up my clothes and returned to the bathroom to get dressed.

"Are we meeting Kenzie and Harper?" I called

119

through the open door.

"No, they're still asleep."

"Okay." I cringed at myself in the mirror. I really hated wearing dresses. Didn't Jack buy me anything else? "Ready?"

"Yep."

"Where's Ryder?"

"Golf with your dad and all the boys."

So that was where Linc disappeared to. "That's the only reason you want to have lunch, isn't it? Ryder's busy, and you're bored," I teased as we stepped into the elevator.

"No, of course not," she gasped. "I just wanted to talk to you about Linc." Her giggle was infectious. Bailey was one of those people who was brimming with happiness all the time—at least since Ryder came along like her own knight in skinny jeans and stole her heart—and if she was smiling, so were you.

"Urgh. I don't want to talk about him."

"The plan to sweep him off his feet isn't working?"

"No, I'm just making a fool of myself." I sighed and followed Bailey out of the elevator as soon as the doors slid open. "Where are we eating?"

"Thought we'd go to the restaurant. It's after the lunch rush, so it should be fairly quiet."

Quiet was good. I wasn't really in the mood for a lot of people. I wasn't even sure I was hungry.

Bailey grabbed us a table at the front, thanking the waitress for the menus.

"Tell me about Linc." She flipped open her menu and scanned it, no doubt for the chicken salad she ordered everywhere we ate. I would have sworn she didn't eat anything else. Her eyes lit up, and I knew she'd found her meal.

"There's nothing to tell. He's Linc, and I'm a hopeless idiot." I groaned and skimmed the menu. I'd get a salad. *Ha*, who was I kidding? Pizza. I wanted a pizza.

The waitress chose that moment to see if we were ready. We gave her our orders, and she returned a moment later with a pitcher of water for the table.

I poured us both a glass and guzzled mine down in two gulps. The heat was killing me. I couldn't wait to get off this island.

"So..." Bailey pressed.

"Nothing."

"Indie?"

"You're not going to let this go, are you?" I folded my arms over my chest and leaned back in the chair.

Bailey shook her head.

"Fine."

I told her everything while we ate, from falling asleep together while we watched *Saw*, and how he held me in his arms all night, him skinny-dipping at the waterfall, dancing at the club, the body shots—she happily pointed out that she was a witness to that sexy moment—and him giving me water and painkillers and staying with me last night to make sure I was okay after drinking so much.

"I don't see the problem." Bailey set her fork down and wiped her mouth with her napkin.

"The problem is, after every one of these

moments, he's dropped a comment that has made me feel like crap. Like last night, telling you there was nothing intimate about doing body shots with me. Well, sorry, but it was. It meant something to me, and it hurt that he brushed it aside so easily. It's just like my eighteenth birthday all over again."

"I don't understand." Bailey frowned in sympathy.

"When he laughed off my first kiss as if it never happened. He does it every time things get a little too close for comfort. I swear, it's like he enjoys messing with my head."

"I don't think that's it."

"What else could it be?"

"Lots of things. I've been watching him this week—"

"Of course, you have." I winked, referring to her walking into his room when he was changing. "Does Ryder know about that?"

"Of course he does. He wasn't too impressed, but I made it up to him," she said.

"Gross." I stuck my finger in my mouth and gagged.

"Not like that." She shook her head in defeat. "Anyway, I've been paying attention to Linc this week, and I think he does these stupid things because he's confused."

"Confused?"

"About you. His feelings. Your feelings. Nate's feelings."

"Umm—"

"Hi, girls. What are you doing here?" I looked up to see my dad standing over the table with a smile, ending our conversation quickly. Maybe Bailey was right and Linc was confused about everything. I could only hope that was the reason and he wasn't brushing me off just because he was a jerk.

"Dad." I stood and kissed his cheek. "Just having lunch. Where's Mum?"

"Spa day."

"Oh, that'd be awesome right now."

"Why don't you girls head over to the spa and join her?"

"Really?"

"Of course."

"Thanks, Dad."

"Thanks, Mr. Kellerman." Bailey smiled.

"Have fun!" He walked off to wherever it was he was going.

"So, spa?" I asked Bailey. We didn't have a lot of time before I had those stupid dance lessons, but we might fit in a facial or something.

"Yes!" She clapped her hands. "I would love a massage."

"Ladies." Jack's voice sounded from behind me. I rolled my eyes. Bailey looked up with a bright smile, so I knew Ryder was there with him too.

"Thought you guys were playing golf?" I said.

"We finished, and your dad bought us lunch. What are you two doing?" Jack slid into the seat beside me and threw his arm around my shoulder, but before I could answer, he kissed me. "Mmmm, still a C." He laughed.

"Jerk." I hit him in the chest.

"You love me."

"Not much, at the moment."

123

"What? Really, baby cakes, I'm heartbroken." He gave me his puppy dog eyes and looked so sad I almost I forgave him for doing this to me. "What have I done?"

"What haven't you done?" I leaned forward and rested my chin in my hands, dreaming about hot stone massages and facials.

"She's feeling—" Bailey spoke.

"Nothing." I glared at her, but she only ignored me.

"Rejected," she said then mouthed *sorry* at me, but she wasn't sorry. She wouldn't let this damn thing go, and if she didn't let it go, Jack wouldn't either. And if they didn't, I'd never get over Linc, and I needed to get over Linc once and for all. All this back and forth and confusion wasn't worth the pain in my chest every time he walked away.

I studied Jack. Maybe taking him up on that offer and handing him my V-card, as he so eloquently put it, wouldn't be such a terrible thing. He was Jack. I loved him dearly, and I knew he loved me, albeit in a platonic way, but at least I knew where I stood with him. He'd do anything for me as well; that much was obvious. He was going to all this trouble just to help me win the affections of someone who didn't give a crap.

But then I looked at Linc—who just appeared at the bar with Nate, making my heart stutter in my chest—and I couldn't imagine being with anyone other than him. It had always been him. My entire life had been about Lincoln Bloody Andrews. The way he smiled. The way he touched his hair, and the way his eyes crinkled at the corners when he laughed. The way he looked in a swimsuit, shorts and tank, a suit—in anything, really. The way he always came to my rescue. The way he played with me growing up when no one else would. The way he stood up for me when Nate threw my teddy bear out of the treehouse window into the mud. I had cried for days because it was ruined, until he showed up with a brand new one he'd bought with his own pocket money because he didn't want me to be sad. The way he picked flowers from the old witch's house down the road, risking being turned into a toad just to cheer me up when I lost the spelling bee at school. It had always been Linc.

It would always be Linc.

Dammit! There was no getting over him. No moving on. I was doomed to spend my life pining for a guy who didn't want me.

"Plans for the afternoon?" Jack asked.

Bailey looked at Ryder, and he lifted a shoulder nonchalantly. "Whatever you want."

"Bailey and I were going to the spa with Mum."

"Oh, okay. Looks like it's just you and me, Ryder buddy." Jack laughed.

"Piss off," he said to Jack and turned to Bailey. "Don't make me spend the day with him, please?"

"You're lucky you've got a nice ass, Jones, otherwise I wouldn't put up with you," Jack said. He loved making fun of Ryder. Any chance he got to tell Ryder how good looking he was, he took it and ran with it, making Ryder uncomfortable.

"Suck it up, baby. We're having a girls' afternoon." Bailey laughed at Jack's comment before kissing Ryder quickly and standing to leave.

"You guys wanna go surfing?" Nate called from over at the bar to Ryder and Jack.

"Yeah." Ryder stood. "Sounds good."

"I hate surfing," Jack huffed.

"They'll all be shirtless," I whispered in his ear.

"Let's go, fellas. What are we waiting for?" He jumped out of his chair and wrapped an arm around Ryder's shoulder.

"Get off me." Ryder ducked out of his hold while Bailey and I stood back and laughed at the whole situation.

"Bye, baby cakes." Jack spun around and winked at me before pressing his lips to my...forehead. Not what I was expecting, but that was fine by me.

The boys left, and Bailey and I made our way outside and across the grounds to the other side of the hotel where the spa was located and went in search of my mother.

CHAPTER FOURTEEN

Linc

It might have been the best surf I'd ever had, except for trying to teach Jack-ass how to stay on the board. I'd never seen anyone so uncoordinated and terrible in the water. Teaching Indie when she was thirteen had been easier. Ryder picked it up quickly. He seemed to have a natural ability in the water, but Jack...I wanted to drown him...on many occasions.

The water was beautiful, crystal clear and warm. I should have gone surfing sooner. I didn't know why I left it so long. No, that was a lie. I knew. Indie. Normally, I'd go for a surf at dawn, but I'd spent the last two nights sleeping beside Indie, not wanting to leave in the morning until I absolutely had to.

I was the only one in the water when Kenzie and Indie showed up on the beach. I wouldn't have known they were there if Indie hadn't put her fingers in her mouth and whistled. It was a talent,

127

that was for sure. She could be heard over the loudest of sounds, even the waves rushing in my ears. I paddled back to the shore and wedged my board in the sand.

Wringing the water out of my hair, I turned to Indie. "What's up?"

"You guys have to get dressed." She pointed at me and Nate, her eyes lingering on my chest—which I may have puffed out somewhat when I noticed her looking—before bringing her gaze back up to meet mine. "Meet us in the ballroom in fifteen minutes."

"Us?" Nate stood and brushed the sand from his shorts.

"Yes, us. Kenzie is your dancing partner." Indie smiled widely while Kenzie groaned.

I raised an eyebrow, and Nate tilted his head, studying Kenzie. "You are?"

"Unfortunately. Only because my brother doesn't want you dancing with Bailey. So I got roped into it." She flicked her blonde hair over her shoulder and looked anything but impressed. She was so much like Ryder, it was freaky.

We left them on the beach and headed back up to our rooms for a quick shower and change of clothes. We were having dinner with the Kellermans after our dance lesson. I was nervous. I didn't dance, not really. I'd only danced twice in my life, one of those times being with Indie last night. The other time? With Indie at her prom. She was the only one who could get me to dance. It was ironic because she wasn't much of a dancer, either.

***

The ballroom was something else. Floor-to-ceiling windows looked out over the resort, gold curtains lined the other walls, polished floorboards, a stage to the right that looked set up for an orchestra, detailed artwork, intricate gold panelling on the walls between the curtains. Crystal chandeliers—not one, but nine of them—put the room in a soft glow. I was impressed. It almost made me want to dance.

"This is where we are having our reception after the ceremony," Leanne announced proudly, spreading her arms out wide and twirling in a small circle. "What do you think?"

"It's beautiful." Indie smiled and gazed around the room in awe. Her face lit with emotions I couldn't decipher.

"I'm glad you like it. Now, we only have tonight for this lesson, but I promise it's not hard. It's just a waltz, and anyone can do that."

Kenzie coughed, and I muttered, "Doubt it." There was no way I could master the waltz after only one lesson.

"Where's the dance instructor?" Indie asked, drawing attention to the fact that there were only the six of us in the ballroom.

"Right here." Kenzie raised her hand and stepped forward.

"You?" Indie said abruptly. "Sorry. I mean, I didn't know you danced."

"Twelve years, until douche-face knocked me up and kicked me out of town." Kenzie shrugged. She was honest, straight to the point, like her brother.

"How is Cole?" Indie asked.

"He's great. He's loving school. Very smart, like his uncle." Kenzie beamed as she spoke about her son. She'd had him when she was about sixteen, I thought Indie had said.

She'd dated Ryder's friend Chace, fell pregnant, and he dumped her, demanding she terminate the baby, which she obviously didn't do. He then went on to date Bailey, knowing Ryder was in love with her, only to dump her for Christina, Bailey and Indie's friend. He was a real piece of work and deserved every single beating Ryder had given him over the years. I knew one thing for sure. I didn't envy Chace being on Ryder's bad side. He might not look it, but the guy was tough. I wouldn't like to piss him off, and I could hold my own in a fight.

"Well, umm…shall we get started?" Steve cleared his throat and looked around awkwardly.

"Yes, please!"

"Okay." Kenzie pulled everyone into a line, with me between Indie and Nate, and stood a few feet in front of us. "I guess we'll start with the basic square. Indie, you watch me. Guys, I'll help you in a minute."

Thank God, because watching her step in a square was confusing the hell out of me.

"One, two, three. One, two, three. Got it?" Kenzie asked Indie, and Indie gave her a thumb up, continuing her steps. "Think you can show Linc?"

"S-sure," she stuttered nervously.

"Remember he has to step in the opposite way, so you lead him. I think it'll be easier," Kenzie said and turned to Leanne and Steve. "If you two want to dance, go for it. Don't wait for us. Watching you will probably help."

"Okay, thank you." Leanne ginned, a smile not unlike her daughter's, before grabbing Steve and pulling him into the middle of the dance floor where they fell into a seamless waltz. Really, they looked like they were floating. I had no hope.

"You ready?" Indie asked.

"Sure." I widened my eyes and smiled awkwardly.

"Okay, boys, I'll run through it with you as we do it this first time. Step forward with your left foot, bring your right foot forward but do not put it down, step it to the side. Good! Bring your left foot over to your right and put it down, step back with the right. Yes! Now bring the left foot back toward the right but slide it to the side. And then bring your right foot over to the left. See, easy? Now, do it together."

It wasn't easy. Far from it. I kept stumbling over my feet, standing on Indie's toes, putting my foot down when it was supposed to glide, stepping with the wrong one. How could anyone ever learn this dance? It was impossible. I looked over to see Nate and Kenzie had finally started waltzing around the room with his parents. He was a natural. I, however, was not. Put me in the water, and I could master anything, but dancing? No.

"Can we try something?" Indie asked, blowing a strand of hair out of her face.

"Anything, if it'll help figure this out." I tugged on my hair, pulling more dreadlocks free.

Indie walked around behind me. "I'm going to lead you from here."

"What?" How could she lead me from behind if I couldn't watch her feet to follow?

Her arms wrapped around my waist, and I froze. What was she doing? Her family would see. Her face was pressed into my back, and I was sure she sniffed. Did she just smell me? Not that I cared. No, I liked it. A little too much. I closed my eyes and waited.

Her left leg nudged mine, so following her lead I moved it forward, then let her guide my right foot forward. When I placed it on the ground, she growled and kicked it to the right. I chuckled, placing my hands on her arms to hold them there, in case she had any ideas of letting me go. She swept my left foot across to my right with hers and stood on my toe when I didn't let it touch the ground. I felt her getting frustrated with me, but I didn't care; I was enjoying having her pressed against my back far too much to care about anything else.

Warms hands wrapped around my arms and pulled them away from Indie's. Frowning, I opened my eyes, expecting to see Nate glaring at me, but it was Kenzie. Pulling my eyebrows together in confusion, I asked, "What are you doing?"

"Helping, 'cause you sure as hell will never figure this out otherwise." She smiled sweetly and placed one of my hands on her shoulder and the other on her waist. I heard Nate's rumbling laughter from the other side of the room. Looking over Kenzie's shoulder, I flipped him off, which only made him laugh harder.

I was glad Ryder wasn't here to see me with my hands on his sister. But with Kenzie leading me from the front, and Indie kicking my feet in the right direction every time I messed up, I managed to complete four full squares. Sure, it took three of us for a two-person dance, but I did it.

"This is like *Dirty Dancing*." Indie laughed into my back.

Kenzie snickered. "Only we're dancing with Linc and not Patrick Swayze, who had the best moves."

"Never seen it," I admitted, feeling like a puppet being led around by two women, one of which I would gladly let lead me around by the balls for the rest of my life, if things weren't so complicated.

"You've never seen it?" Kenzie raised an eyebrow in disbelief. I shook my head.

"We're changing that, soon," Indie announced.

Whatever. If I watched it with her, I didn't have a problem. Hell, I'd watch *The Notebook* if she wanted me to.

"Sure, Princess."

"Okay, I think you two are good to go on your own now. Wanna give it a go?" Kenzie stepped back, giving Indie room to come around to my front. I rested one hand on her shoulder gently and gripped her hip with the other, pulling her closer to my body than I had Kenzie because, well, it was Indie, and I wanted her close all the time.

"Ready?" She smiled brightly.

"Let's do it."

And we did. Perfectly. Kenzie clapped, while Nate cheered us on, jumping around like a baboon.

We danced for an hour, eventually figuring out how to move around the dance floor and not in a tiny square. We were far from graceful, but at least we had the steps right. Finally.

But I'd practice all night if it meant dancing with Indie in my arms a little longer.

I was a sucker for punishment.

CHAPTER FIFTEEN

Indie

We had dinner on the roof. I didn't even know there was a rooftop bar and restaurant, but the food was delicious, and the evening was warm. Kenzie didn't join us for dinner, saying she didn't want to leave Harper alone with Jack for too long, which was understandable. So, it was just Mum, Dad, Nate, Linc, and me. Just like old times. Only things felt too tense now.

Mum and Dad quizzed me on school and wanted to know more about Jack—they seemed to really like him—making me feel terribly guilty for lying about our relationship, or lack of one. They asked about the house I shared with Bailey and Ryder, and I screwed up by mentioning I lived with Jack as well, not thinking they'd take that the wrong way because they believed we were in a relationship.

Dad choked on his beer. "You're living with your boyfriend?"

"I thought your other roommate—I can't

remember his name—was gay?" my mother asked.

"You have separate bedrooms, right?" Nate growled.

And Linc was silent. Like always. Fingers clenched around the knife again.

"Yes, I'm living with Jack and in separate rooms," I reassured them, feeling a little better because at least none of that was a lie. "Bailey and Ryder are there all the time. It's fine, really."

After the first shock of that little tidbit wore off, dinner went smoothly. It was nice to catch up and do something as a family like we did growing up. It reminded me so much of our Sunday night dinners. Linc would join us, and we'd spend the night eating and talking. I hadn't realised how much I had missed my family until now.

After we'd eaten, my parents said goodnight and left. It was getting late. Nate yawned and announced he was heading back to his room as well. I guessed he was still tired after being out all the night before. "What about you guys?"

"I think we might take advantage of the band," Linc pointed to the two-man band in the corner of the roof, "and practise that dance a little longer. What do you think?" he asked me.

"You need all the help you can get." I smiled and stood, dropping my bag on the table.

"Don't leave that there. Someone will steal it." Linc picked it up and handed it to Nate. "Take this back for her."

"Okay. Good luck with the moves, man. You're gonna need it." He laughed, waving over his shoulder as he walked off.

"Come on." Linc grabbed my hand and pulled me over to the makeshift dance floor, a square space free of tables and chairs.

We danced the waltz for so long my feet felt like they were on fire and my arms were too heavy to lift.

"Again," Linc said, gripping my waist and pulling me closer. Thunder rumbled overhead. I looked up at the sky and noticed all the stars had disappeared.

"I think it's going to rain," I said.

"One more time. Please, Indie," he pleaded.

"Okay."

No sooner had we taken a step than the rain started, hard and fast. But Linc made us finish our loop around the dancefloor before pulling me into the stairwell.

We took the stairs carefully, making sure not to slip because they were all wet from every other person on the roof escaping the rain. Once were reached the top floor, we had to wait for the elevator to come back up and get us.

"Hope it doesn't rain for the wedding," Linc said, wiping water from his face. His shirt clung to him, accentuating each and every muscle on his torso. He looked like a god. And I looked like a drowned rat. I frowned at my appearance in the mirror beside the elevator doors. Smoothing my hands over my face and hair didn't help at all.

The doors opened, and we took the lift downstairs, only to realise we had to run to our building through the rain. By the time we got upstairs to our rooms, we were saturated. And...

"Dammit!" I banged my head on my door.

"What?" Linc asked with an amused smile.

"Nate has my key and my phone. Again. I can't believe I did it again."

"I'll let you through to your room from mine."

"Thanks."

I followed him into his room and over to the door that separated our rooms, but it wouldn't open.

"What the hell?" Linc said, trying again.

"Use your key," I suggested helpfully.

Grabbing his key card out of his wallet, he looked at the door handle. "There's no slot for the card. Dammit, look. It needs an actual key. Did you lock it from your side?"

"No." I shook my head, confused about how it got locked when I knew I hadn't done it, not since I unlocked it last night after the club.

"I'll call Nate."

"Okay." I shivered, the rain well and truly seeping into my bones now.

"Shit, sorry, Princess. Go dry yourself off. There are spare towels in the bathroom."

"Thanks." I left him to call Nate and went in search of clean, dry towels.

Peeling my wet dress off was a great idea. I felt warmer at once without the cold, wet fabric sticking to my skin. Grabbing a towel from under the sink, I squeezed the excess water from my hair down the drain and then rubbed the towel through the ends.

"He's not answering, but—" Linc's voice stopped immediately.

I looked over my shoulder at him, staring wide-eyed. Crap. I didn't lock the door. Holding the

138

towel in one hand, I was frozen to the spot. Linc was shirtless. In fact, he didn't have pants on either. Clearly having the same idea as me about getting out of wet clothes, he was standing there in only his boxers.

He didn't move. He didn't speak. And neither did I. I didn't know what to do. Yell at him for walking in on me in only my underwear—thankfully, black this time, and not see-through at all? Wrap a towel around me so he couldn't see anything? But that would be stupid. He'd seen it all when we went swimming yesterday. Instead, I stood there like an idiot and waited for him to leave.

Why wasn't he leaving?

He pinched his bottom lip between his fingers and stepped farther into the bathroom. And still I didn't move. His grey eyes were so much darker than before, and his gaze travelled down my body deliberately before coming back up and resting on my face.

Another step closer.

And another.

He was directly in front of me, so close the heat from his body warmed me. His fingers wrapped around the towel and plucked it from my hands. Taking one step behind me, I moved my gaze to the mirror to watch him as he rubbed the towel over my wet skin. Across my shoulder blades, down my arms, dragging painfully slow. Goose bumps erupted on my skin everywhere he touched. I watched his hand travel across my stomach, around my back. My breath stopped when he brought the towel over my chest and down across my hips before pulling my hair over one shoulder and wrapping the white cloth around the end of my locks.

I watched him as he watched me.

I watched the towel fall from his fingers to the floor.

I watched his hands skim over my stomach, tickle my ribs.

I watched him kiss my shoulder, his lips barely grazing the skin and sliding along to where my neck and shoulder met. My breath caught in my throat.

What was he doing?

My eyes drifted closed, and my head fell to the side. This was too much. I couldn't handle it. I had wanted this for so long, and now I didn't know what to do. What did it mean? Did it mean anything? Or would he just brush it off as nothing again? If he turned into a jerk again, it'd be the end of me. I'd pack my bags and get on the next plane out of here, wedding or no wedding. I couldn't keep going back and forth, not when he did things like this.

My legs were like jelly. They could barely support my weight as I struggled to catch my breath. He literally knocked the air out of me, simply by kissing my oversensitive skin. I'd wanted his lips on me again, ever since my eighteenth birthday, but I never imagined it would have me feeling that way—so nervous, excited, scared. All these emotions bubbled inside me, and I was struggling to maintain my calm.

His nose dragged along my skin, up my neck to where he placed a kiss behind my ear and groaned my name. Shivers ran up my spine.

"I'll get you something to wear," he said, meeting my gaze in the mirror. If I wasn't mistaken, he looked like he was in pain, confused, like he didn't know what to do. He was struggling with whatever this was between us as much as I was. I just wished I knew what he was struggling with. Was it because we shouldn't be this close? Or was it—hopefully—that he wanted more too and was just as unsure as I was about this? No, he'd never be unsure. He was the one person I knew who always seized the moment and went for whatever it was he wanted. But this time he looked so uncertain. His eyes were guarded, hesitant.

He squeezed my waist and placed one last kiss against my jaw and walked out of the bathroom, leaving me to fall in a heap against the counter.

Hell.

I was done for.

A couple of minutes later, he returned with a white tank for me. That was it. No shorts? Not even a t-shirt? Just one of those tanks with the wide armholes. "Thanks."

"I'll give you a minute," he said quietly and walked back out of the room that felt increasingly smaller with each passing second.

I slide the shirt over my head and ran my fingers through my hair to try to get some of the tangles out, but it was futile.

Returning to the room, I found Linc lying on the bed with the television paused on the beginning scene of *Dirty Dancing*.

"Thought we could watch this?"

"Okay." I shuffled on my feet and twisted the

hem of his tank between my fingers. My nerves were shot. We'd never done anything like that before. And everything I'd thought was intense and meaningful up until tonight paled in comparison to that moment in the bathroom. And what was even harder to wrap my head around was that Linc was acting normal. He wasn't brushing it aside as if it were nothing. He was simply behaving like he towel-dried me and kissed my neck all the time.

"Indie?" He patted the bed beside him.

I walked over slowly and paused at the edge of the bed, unsure about how I felt lying next to him now. Would he expect something else? Would I expect something else?

I didn't get to dwell on it for too long, though, because he reached for my hand and pulled me down beside him, wrapping an arm around my back until my head was settled comfortably against his chest.

"You know, as hot as you look in your lace underwear, I think I prefer you in my clothes," he said softly, pressing *play* on the movie and tracing soft circles on the bare skin of my hip, because obviously his tank had ridden up the moment I lay down.

CHAPTER SIXTEEN

Linc

I woke in the morning wrapped around Indie, legs tangled together, my head on her chest, and one hand on her breast. I knew I should move, that I shouldn't have been holding her like that, but I didn't want to. I was going to enjoy every moment of it until she moved or woke up.

I'd lost my mind last night when I saw her standing in the bathroom in her underwear. It wasn't any different than when we went swimming at the waterfall, but last night something in me snapped. I didn't care that what I was doing broke all sorts of codes and friendship rules. I didn't care about anything but getting closer to Indie. I thought I realised, or had at least finally made up my mind, that she was worth risking everything for. I just had to be sure she felt the same way.

But it was hard to figure out because she had a boyfriend. Who never slept in her room, here or at home. She'd spent every night with me so far instead of him. Something didn't add up. Why was she sleeping with me if she had a boyfriend? Why didn't he care that she was spending more time with me than with him? All these questions and I didn't know how to answer them.

Indie woke up a little while later. I could always tell when she woke but pretended to be asleep. She used to do it all the time, hugging me closer—I let myself believe it was because she didn't want me to leave, that she didn't want to let me go. I was motionless, hand still comfortably on her breast, and waited for her to move, to shift in some way that caused me to drop my hand, but she didn't. She didn't move at all. I didn't know what that meant. There were so many possibilities. Maybe she didn't want to risk waking me if she thought I was asleep, or maybe she liked that I was holding her like this.

Her fingers danced along my back up and up into my hair, twisting and twirling a dreadlock, yet she still didn't move or push my hand away. I was going to enjoy every second until it came to an end—

My phone rang from the other side of the room and ruined the moment. Faking a yawn and a stretch, Indie pretended to wake up, shifting under me so I had to roll away.

"Morning, Princess. How'd you sleep?"

"Mmmm, great. You?"

"Better than ever." I stretched out beside her.

"You gonna get that?"

"No."

"It could be important. Could be Nate wanting to bring my key up."

144

"You don't need your key. You're here."

"I can't stay in my underwear and your top all day, Lincoln." She was cute when she tried to scold me.

"You won't hear any complaints from me." I laughed, rolling off the bed when my phone rang again. "Yeah," I answered gruffly, disappointed that I had to get up.

"Hey." Dammit. It was Nate. "I just saw your call and realised I had Indie's room key all night, didn't I?"

"Yeah." I ran a hand over my face and tried to wake myself up a little better.

"Where is she?"

"Here."

"With you?" he asked, a challenging tone to his voice.

"No, I let her sleep in the hallway. Of course, she's here with me."

"Okay, I'm on my way up," he said and hung up.

"Nate's coming." I threw the phone down on the bed and grabbed a pair of shorts and t-shirt for Indie to wear instead. "As much as I like the view, you should put on something a little more modest so Nate doesn't freak out."

"Thanks." She smiled and climbed out of the bed to do the one thing I didn't expect her to do. She pulled the tank off, right in front of me. My mouth went dry instantly.

"Dammit, Indie." I stepped around the bed until I was face to face with her.

"What?" She raised her eyebrows innocently.

"You're walking a very fine line right now," I

ground out through a clenched jaw. We were chest to chest.

"It's not like you haven't seen it a thousand times already this week. What's the point of hiding in the bathroom?" Her breath was rapid.

Valid.

"Because I'm barely controlling myself right now," I whispered against her cheek. Pulling back, I reached one hand up and touched the base of her throat, spreading my fingers out over her collarbone. I felt the beat of her heart beneath my palm, getting faster and faster with every second.

I dragged my hand tenderly down her chest, over the swell of her breasts, and across her flat stomach until I gripped her hips, and I pulled her even closer to me. "Better be careful, Princess, or I might do something that'll get us both in all sorts of trouble," I said, thinking that would be the end of this torturous game she was playing. But I couldn't have been more wrong.

"Well…" She licked her lips. When did she get to be so seductive? She was always seductive to me, but when did she get so good at it? "Maybe I want you too."

And with that, she stepped back and went into the bathroom to get changed.

I groaned and fell onto the bed. What the hell was she doing? What did that mean?

Reaching for the phone, I called the front desk for our complimentary room service and internally kicked myself when Indie came back into the room wearing my shorts and t-shirt. Was it too much to ask that she never wore anything other than one of my tanks ever again?

Room service arrived before Nate did, so we managed to enjoy half our breakfast on the balcony in peace. I expected things to be weird between us, a little awkward after all the flirting in the last twelve hours, but it wasn't. We both simply relaxed.

I had just grabbed a bagel when there was a knock at the door. "That'll be Nate."

I answered the door and was disappointed to find not only Nate, but Jack-ass as well. "Ooh, bagel." He clapped excitedly and took the bagel from my hand and headed straight to the balcony where Indie was wearing my clothes. Mine. Not his. I was a little smug about that.

"Baby cakes." He really announced his presence no matter where he went. He was so loud and obnoxious. I didn't see what Indie found appealing about him at all.

"Sorry, man. Thanks for giving her a place to crash," Nate said as we walked outside just in time to see Jack about suck Indie's face off. Where was that knife?

I didn't know how much more I could handle watching him all over her every time they were together.

I needed to come clean about my feelings, but I'd wait until after the wedding tomorrow because I didn't want to ruin it before it happened. At least I was considerate.

"So what's the plan for today?" Jack asked, stealing an apple from the cart.

"I really just want to lounge by the pool or on the beach. I want a relaxing day," Indie said as she poured a cup of coffee and added half a sugar. She handed it to me. Me. Not Jack-ass, her boyfriend. My chest might have puffed up a little bit at that.

"Sounds good," Nate agreed, while Jack mumbled something that sounded like "yes." But I was too focused on Indie, imagining her in her swimsuit.

"I'm definitely keen." I gazed at her, making her cheeks heat up in embarrassment.

"Great. We'll meet you down there in half an hour, then," Jack said, pulling Indie out of the chair and throwing her over his shoulder. "Better make it an hour." He winked and carried her inside, completely ignoring her protests and cries to put her down.

"I really hate that guy," I mumbled to Nate.

He barked out a laugh and clapped me on the back. "Of course, you do."

"What's that supposed to mean?" I frowned.

"That you've hated any guy who has ever paid her any attention. You've always put a stop to it, but this time it's worse because you weren't there to stop this train wreck of a relationship from happening."

"Just looking out for her. Don't want her to end up with an asshole." I left out the part about wanting her to be with me.

"Or anyone else," Nate muttered.

"What?"

"Nothing, I'll go tell the others we'll meet them at the pool in an hour," he said and left.

CHAPTER SEVENTEEN

Indie

"You really need to stop throwing me over your shoulder every time we leave a room together," I hissed at Jack the moment he put me on my feet in my room.

"But it's so much fun seeing him all riled up. He hates it when I manhandle you."

"So do I," I said and went straight over to the door that joined the two rooms and unlocked it. Jack threw his head back and laughed.

"Did you do that?" I asked, pointing at the door.

"Of course not! I'm offended that you could even suggest such a thing. But Bailey…"

So that was why she hung around yesterday while I got ready for lunch. What else did she do?

"You two are incredible!"

"Why, thank you." Jack placed a hand delicately on his chest and tilted his head down with a shy

149

smile.

"Not a compliment."

"Maybe not to you. So?"

"So, what?" I knew what he wanted, but I wasn't giving details that easily.

"What happened last night?"

"N-nothing."

"That doesn't sound like nothing." Jack opened my suitcase and began rifling through it. "Spill."

"Nothing. We danced, got caught in the rain, and watched a movie."

"*Dirty Dancing*?"

"Yes." I angled my head to the side. "How did you know we watched that?"

"What? No," he said before ripping something out of my case excitedly. "Aha! I meant did you dirty dance together, not the movie. You actually watched that?"

"Yes. No. I mean—*grrr,* you're so confusing sometimes. No, we didn't dirty dance together. We waltzed, in the rain. And, yes, we did watch that movie. Linc's never seen it."

"I bet he looks mighty fine dripping wet in the rain." Jack raised his eyebrows at me.

"Well, duh."

"And then what?"

"Nothing."

"You're lying." He narrowed his eyes and threw a bikini in my face.

"He kissed me," I muttered and turned to walk into the bathroom, hoping to escape Jack before he realised what I said.

"He *what*?" Jack screeched as he followed me

150

into the bathroom.

"It was nothing. He just walked into the bathroom, much like you right now, and took the towel from me and dried my skin then kissed my shoulder a little."

"A little?"

"Maybe my neck too." I felt the heat creeping into my cheeks. Why I found it so hard to talk about, I didn't know, but it was embarrassing. Possibly because Jack tended to overreact.

"Yes! Baby cakes, this is what we've been waiting for our whole lives!" Jack wrapped his arms around me and spun excitedly. Overreacting.

"We?"

"Yes, we. I've dreamed about a guy like Linc forever, so I'm living vicariously through you. Tell me more."

"There's nothing else to tell. We fell asleep, and I woke to find his hand, umm…"

"Umm?"

"Here." I held my hand in front of my chest.

"He grabbed a fun bag?" Jack grinned.

"A what?" I asked, sure my face looked as shocked as I felt.

"A fun bag."

"What are fun bags?"

I regretted asking at once. Particularly asking Jack, the one person who didn't have boundaries.

"These, baby cakes." He reached out and grabbed my breasts with both hands.

"Stop. What are you doing?" I tried to push his hands away, but it only made him squeeze them more.

"Playing with your fun bags," he said and laughed.

"Why?"

"Because they're fun, Indie, hence the name," he said, jiggling them in his hands.

"Okay, enough now, please." I squirmed.

Jack dropped his hands in defeat. "Just trying to help."

"Well, stop. I don't need it."

"A solid C, remember?"

"Have I told you how much I hate you?" I grabbed him by the shoulders and shoved him out of the bathroom.

He poked his head back through the door. "Nope. Because you love me. I know it."

"Don't get too cocky."

He turned serious all of a sudden. "You know this plan of mine is going to work, right?"

"Hmmm." I wasn't sure what I thought about his plan anymore.

"Baby cakes, I love you, and I want you to be happy. Trust me?"

"Of course. But I feel wrong about lying to everyone."

"No one needs to know we're lying. Except for Linc when you two finally hook up."

"We are not hooking up." Oh God, what if that's all Linc saw me as? A hook up. All this flirting and back and forth, what if he only wanted sex? I wanted more. I wanted everything. I couldn't just be another girl, someone to pass the time while he was on holidays.

"You're overthinking." Jack rubbed his thumb

between my eyes. "You'll get wrinkles if you keep frowning like that. 'Hook up' might have been a bad choice of words. You don't want to start off your relationship with Linc on a lie. You'll have to tell him the truth, but no one else needs to know."

"Relationship?"

"Yes. That's why we're doing this whole charade. Now quit wasting time and trying to use your womanly wiles to make me straight." He winked and pulled the door closed, giving me a moment of quiet to change into my swimsuit, if it could be called that. Pretty sure it was missing a piece or six. What on earth would that cover?

I grabbed a robe from behind the door to cover myself up with once I was changed. Seriously, my underwear covered more than that bikini. "You didn't happen to buy me some board shorts to go with this, did you?" I asked Jack the moment I was back in the room.

"How could you even ask such a question?" He smiled. Hope blossomed in my stomach. He had something I would be comfortable wearing. "Of course not! You're not going to win Adonis's heart by dressing like him."

"Adonis?"

"I think it's more fitting than Linc."

"Right, well, for your information, Linc told me he prefers me in his tank than my clothes, anyway," I responded with a smug smile. If I knew it wouldn't start an immaturity war, I would have stuck my tongue out at him.

"Well, of course, he does. Seeing you in his clothes automatically makes him think about waking up next to you. Which in turn makes him think about you sleeping next to him. Which then leads to him thinking about ripping your clothes off and having his way with you, ultimately leaving you no choice but to wear his clothes to bed." Jack opened the door and stepped into the hallway.

"He thinks about having sex with me?" I choked on air, gasping for breath. Hook up. Hook up. Hook up.

"About every three seconds of the day."

I eyed him sceptically.

"Scout's honour. It's a guy thing. Trust me, I know. I am one."

"Right. Let's just go and meet the others."

I didn't want to discuss Linc with Jack anymore. All he did was make me panic and cause me to worry more.

***

The pool was quiet when we got outside, except for our friends splashing and making so much noise I was concerned someone would come and tell us to be quiet. But no one did. I lay back on one of the deck chairs next to Bailey and Kenzie, making myself comfortable and hoping to get a bit of colour on my skin.

The boys were all in the pool playing with pool toys. Kids' ones. There were pool noodles and kickboards, a beach ball, a floating beanbag, a raft—that Nate was lying on—a blow-up basketball hoop and basketball that Linc and Brody were playing with, and a blow-up seahorse that Ryder was sitting on. Jack kicked off his shoes to join them, running for the pool and jumping straight over Ryder's head, splashing water everywhere.

"Well, looks like they're having fun. Where did they get all that stuff?" I asked.

"Stole it from the kiddie pool over there." Bailey sighed and shook her head.

Of course. And I was willing to bet it had been Nate's idea. He was a big child sometimes. I often wondered which of us was actually older.

I settled back in my chair and closed my eyes, once I realised Bailey had pulled out her book to read, and Kenzie had plugged in her earphones, drowning out all the noise around us. Fine by me. I wanted to relax, maybe have a nap, and this was the perfect way to do it.

Until I woke up as I was flying into the pool. I screamed just before I hit the surface, sucking in air and water at the same time. I came up spluttering and coughing. My chest burned, and my nose stung.

"You okay, baby cakes?" Jack stood on the edge of the pool with an amused smile on his face.

"No, I'm drowning, you idiot."

"Doesn't look like it to me."

"Shut up," I answered maturely and swam to the edge to pull myself out.

"Want to play a game?" Jack asked everyone, pushing me back into the water.

"What?" I was cautious. Jack was unpredictable and could come up with the weirdest games.

"Marco Polo."

"Ha, really?" I asked.

"Yeah, why not? It's fun in the pool. Guys?"

A chorus of *yes* and *sure* followed. So I spent the next two hours playing Marco Polo in a swimming pool filled with accessories for six year olds, with five males in their twenties.

Good times.

CHAPTER EIGHTEEN

Linc

I loved the water. I could have spent the entire day in the pool, but after ten rounds of playing aquatic hide and seek with your eyes closed, I'd had enough of Marco Polo. We had to return all the toys to the kids' pool once families started coming out for a swim, though we did manage to keep the basketball hoop for a little while and get a few games in.

Harper showed up later than the rest of us, and Nate made a beeline for her. The guys had grown tired of swimming and were relaxing on the deck chairs with the girls—Jack was rubbing sunscreen all over Indie, much to my disappointment—when I decided it would be the perfect time to go for a surf. Yesterday was perfect, and I hadn't surfed as much as I wanted to, not that I was complaining when the alternative was spending time with Indie.

157

"I'm going for a surf," I announced and grabbed my towel from the chair. I didn't invite anyone, wanting the peace and quiet at least for a little while.

"Can I come?" Indie called to me.

I turned and walked backwards. "Sure, if you want."

"Great." She stood and started toward me.

"Wait for me, baby cakes. I wouldn't mind a few more lessons." Jack jumped out of the chair and followed.

Clenching my jaw, I chose not to say anything to him. Why was he here again? "Anyone else want to come?"

Thankfully, they all shook their heads, opting to lounge by the pool for the rest of the day.

We grabbed three boards from the kiosk on our way down to the beach and walked along the sand to find a less crowded place. The beach was busier than yesterday, bodies sunbaking everywhere. It took us a while to find somewhere, eventually heading around the point and away from the stretch of beach the hotel was on.

"This is perfect," I said and walked into the water without waiting for Jack and Indie. Indie knew how to surf well enough, so I figured she could give Jack some tips and help him.

The water was warm but refreshing, and the surface was smooth and still until the waves broke. It was the ideal conditions. I paddled out beyond the break and looked over at Indie on the shore giving Jack advice. He was lying on his board in the sand and trying to jump onto his feet. On the flat sand, he wasn't too bad. He got up smoothly and placed his feet in the right position. It was only when he was in the water he seemed to forget what he meant to do.

I left them to it. They'd get in the water when they were ready. Lying on my board, I waited for the next wave. I paddled forward as it approached, climbed to my feet, and slid along the surface of the water, riding the wave all the way to the end. There was no feeling like surfing. It was the ultimate. A rush. It was powerful and addictive. I loved every second of it.

I didn't know how long I surfed, paddling back out, riding the waves back in. Over and over. Indie and Jack came out after a while. Indie managed to stay on the board most of the time. I guessed she was a little rusty. I doubted she surfed much while at uni, if at all. It had probably been a few years, but she did well. And Jack was getting the hang of it, even staying upright on his board a couple of times before wiping out.

Time passed quickly, the adrenaline pumping through my veins. I felt like a king out on the water. Untouchable. It wasn't until I noticed I was out there alone that I realised it was getting late. We had the rehearsal dinner tonight, so I paddled back in, wanting to have a shower and freshen up. I didn't want to be late, because Leanne would kill me.

I was surprised to find Indie sitting on the sand, watching me. "What are you still doing here?"

"I like watching you surf." She smiled, her arms wrapped around her knees. I liked that she liked to watch me. "You make it look so graceful."

"Thanks." I laughed, sitting beside her. "Where's Jack?"

"He went back inside for a sleep. Surfing tired him out."

"Really? It has the opposite effect on me. I'm full of energy now. What time is it?"

"Don't know, but we should head back in and get ready." She stood and brushed the sand from her legs, missing a spot.

"Wait, come here." I grabbed her hips and pulled her to stand in front of me. I reached up and dusted the sand from the tops of her legs and her bikini bottoms, lingering a little longer on her ass than I should have. "There, that's better."

Indie cleared her throat. "Ah, thanks."

I stood and grabbed both boards and carried them back to the kiosk.

"Do you have your key this time?" I joked as we stepped onto the elevator.

She dipped her fingers into her bikini top and pulled out the card for her room with a wink. "Yep!"

I couldn't say I wasn't disappointed she had her key. I liked when she relied on me. I liked coming to her rescue. Mostly because it meant she would spend more time with me.

I said goodbye to Indie at my door and watched her walk into her room. It was 5:30. We had to be in the ballroom at 6:30 for the run-through. I didn't understand why they needed a rehearsal dinner. We sat down, we ate, did speeches, then danced. It wasn't hard.

After I had showered and dressed, I knocked on

160

the door that separated our rooms to see if she was ready to go. I was glad I knocked because as soon as I did, I heard raised voices. More specifically, Jack-ass yelling. I hesitated, unsure whether I should walk in there and see if everything was okay. It was instinct to make sure Indie was safe, to protect her from harm, as natural as breathing.

Jack's voice stopped immediately, and after a few seconds, the door opened to reveal a scowling Indie.

"What?" The tone in her voice shocked me. She'd never spoken to me that way before. Sure, she'd been pissed off at me over the years, snapping at me, yelling, but the venom in her voice this time was different.

"Umm, I just wanted to see if you were ready to go." I rubbed the back of my neck.

"Just give me a minute." Her voice softened, and she smiled apologetically.

"Everything okay?" I looked over her shoulder and glared at Jack.

She answered with a shrug. "Actually, you know what? No, nothing is okay." She pushed the door open to allow me in and turned to Jack. "This is crazy. I'm not doing it anymore. I know you mean well, but this plan you have masterminded is driving me crazy. I'm done. It's finished. And right now, I want to be alone." She snatched her bag from the table and stormed out the door.

What the hell just happened?

Jack groaned, running his hands over his face. "I tried. You can't say I didn't try." He stomped out of the room after Indie, leaving me standing there confused and dumbstruck.

I obviously was missing something, but I didn't know what. What was over? Her and Jack-ass, I could only hope. Mastermind. Plans. None of it made sense.

I returned to my room to get my phone before heading over to the ballroom, still trying to work out what went wrong. The day had been great—at least, I thought so—but now I was sure Indie was crying somewhere to Bailey because of something Jack had said or done.

**

To say the rehearsal dinner was tense would be an understatement. Everyone could sense it. Even Nate's parents looked concerned. Bailey kept looking at Indie as though she were about to break at any moment. Ryder glared at Jack the entire meal, and I sat there trying to make sense of everything.

I wanted to speak to Indie and find out what was going on, make sure she was okay, but she wouldn't even look at me. How could things change in such a short amount of time?

What did Jack do?

I finally got my chance to speak to Indie when it was time for the first dance.

"So, do you want to tell me what's going on?" I asked, stepping in time with her around the dance floor. We certainly didn't glide like Leanne and Steve, but we had the steps right, and for that, I was proud.

"No, not really." She faked a smile. "Everything is fine."

"It's not. What did Jack-ass do?"

"Jack-ass?" She raised a questioning eyebrow.

"Sorry. It's my nickname for him." I smiled.

"You're not sorry."

"Not at all. I don't like him. And I think you should be with someone else," I admitted. Me. I wanted to say me, but I kept my mouth shut.

"We're not together, so don't worry. And you really don't have to hate him. He's not as bad as you think."

They weren't together. Since when? That argument earlier. Did I witness them breaking up?

"Since when?"

"I really don't want to talk about it right now," she insisted.

"Well, I do." I was pushing for more information because I didn't like her being upset, and she was clearly upset about something.

"Look, it doesn't matter."

"Dammit, Indie, tell me." My voice was raising, like it so often did when I was frustrated with her.

"No!" she snapped and dropped her hands from mine, taking a step back. "Just leave it alone, okay?"

She walked away, stopped to apologise to her parents, and ran from the room. Ran from me.

"Indie, get back here," I shouted after her, but she was gone.

All eyes were on me. Brody and Ryder were covering their mouths with their hands, like they knew what was going on. The girls were sitting there with stupid grins. Jack was relaxed in his chair, hands folded behind his head and a smug smile on his face. He looked pretty content for a guy who just broke up with his girlfriend of a year. I looked at Nate, and he simply nodded in the direction Indie went, telling me to go after her. So, after a quick apology to his parents, I ran from the room in search of Indie.

I didn't know where she could have gone. The bar. The pool. Her room. My room. Jack's room. The spa. I checked them all, and then it hit me. The one place other than her treehouse that she loved escaping to when she was younger.

The beach.

CHAPTER NINETEEN

Indie

Everything was quickly spiralling out of control. Jack had come up with a ridiculous plan to start a fight with Linc and make him admit his feelings for me, but I didn't want to ruin my parents' wedding with a fight.

Ha! Look how that turned out. I just stormed out of their rehearsal dinner in tears because Lincoln Bloody Andrews didn't know when to quit.

The sand was still warm from the heat of the day, and the waves crashing against the shore were relaxing. I'd been out here a while and figured he'd show up eventually. He wouldn't stop looking until he found me, but I wasn't sure I was ready to be found yet. I had a feeling things were about to explode; I just hoped it wasn't me left to pick up the pieces of my shattered heart.

"Indie." Linc's deep voice floated through the

breeze, caressing my skin and causing goose bumps on my flesh. Always.

"I told you I didn't want to talk about it." I stood and brushed off the sand, walking to the water to dip my toes in.

"I don't care. You're out here crying on the beach alone. I just want you to be okay."

"Well, I'm not okay. Everything is a mess. Hard. Complicated. I never should have come, but you know, it's my parents. I had to be here, but I really just want to go back to school and get away from…" I trailed off, stopping myself from saying the rest.

"Get away from what?"

"You!" I didn't mean to shout, but it felt good. "This, us. Everything."

He put his hands in his pockets and ducked his head. I'd hurt him. But I was hurting, too. Every time I saw him, I hurt. And now all I could think about was just being a hook up to him.

"Well, go, then. It's not like you ever come home to visit, anyway. Is it because of him? Did he stop you coming back all this time?" Linc refused to look at me, choosing to focus on his foot digging into the sand.

"No, it wasn't him. It's never been about Jack. He's tried to get me to come home. He's the one who forced me here this week." I ran my hands through my hair in frustration.

"Then, why? Why don't you come home? Make me understand."

"Because of you!" I was shouting again. People further down the beach turned in our direction to see what the commotion was, but I didn't care. "It hurt too much. You hurt too much."

"Me? How? What did I do?" He walked away and turned back. *"I did nothing!"*

"That's the problem! For years, nothing! When all I've wanted is you…"

"What?" He stood directly in front of me and placed his hands on my arms.

"I'm in love with you, you stupid ass." I shoved his hands away and stepped around him. It was out in the open now. My heartbeat was going crazy; I could feel it my throat. My hands were trembling as I wiped at the tears dripping down my cheeks.

"Say it again," he said quietly. I turned to look at him, a pained expression on his face, his hands pulling at his dreadlocks.

"You stupid ass."

"Not that bit."

"I'm in love with you," I whispered, my breath catching in my throat.

"Again," he demanded, stepping closer.

"I'm in lo—"

His hands were in my hair and his mouth was on mine, cutting off the rest of my words.

Hard, demanding, urgent. Bliss.

My knees buckled, and I wrapped my arms around his waist to support myself. Stars danced behind my eyelids as he tilted my head back and slipped his tongue between my lips, exploring my mouth, massaging my tongue with his. I groaned and pulled him closer, my fingernails digging into his back. His hands still firmly planted on the side of my face, we kissed. And kissed.

167

He pulled back. "I'm so glad you feel that way, Princess," he murmured against my lips and kissed me again.

"You are?" I asked stupidly when we finally came up for air.

"Yeah, I am." He still had my face in his hands. His eyes, dark grey, a raging storm of emotions, focused entirely on me. "I have loved you forever."

"You're a jerk, you know that?"

"But you love me anyway." He smirked, making my insides melt. I adored that look.

"I've tried really hard not to, but it seems you're too ingrained in me. You're like a bad habit, and I keep going back for more."

"A bad habit you don't want to quit, right?" He wrapped his arms around me, holding me to his chest. In his warm embrace, I felt safe, secure, and right where I should be.

"One I can't quit." I smiled into his shirt, breathing him in. He smelled like the ocean, a scent I would never get tired of.

"One that's going to cause a lot of trouble," he muttered, placing a soft kiss to the top of my head. My stomach fluttered with nerves. He was right. We had to tell my family about us. Even though I didn't know what we were, we couldn't...I couldn't keep lying to them. They'd figure it out eventually, anyway.

I took a deep breath. "Do you think it will be bad?"

"I think Nate is going to weigh down my boots and dump me in the ocean." He laughed humourlessly.

I squeezed him tighter.

"I won't let that happen. I'll talk to him."

"No, I'll do it. It needs to be me. It should be me." His fingers twirled a strand of my hair.

"Together?"

"I'm not going to get my way on this, am I?"

"Nope." I looked up at him and smiled when he lowered his head to kiss me again.

"Fine, but not until after your parents' wedding. I don't want to cause a scene."

"Like we did tonight?" I cringed at what my parents must have thought when I took off. I hoped they weren't upset.

"Yeah, but it was worth it." He sat on the sand and pulled me down to sit between his legs, threading his fingers through mine.

I leaned back into his chest, a sigh escaping my lips. I was happy. Content. And terrified. I didn't know what any of this meant. He loved me, but that didn't mean he wanted to be with me. There were so many obstacles in our way. So many reasons not to take this further.

"I can hear you thinking," he murmured in my ear, bringing our hands up and flipping them over. I was mesmerised by both the movement and the fact we were holding hands like it was the most natural thing in the world, as though we did it every day. "What's up?"

"Just trying to work out what all this means."

"What?"

"You, me. This."

"What do you want it to mean?" He shifted behind me, his voice shaky. He was nervous about my answer.

"What do you want this to mean?" I repeated his question. I'd already admitted my feelings first, so it was only fair he told me what he felt about us. "How do you see this ending?"

"Ending?" His voice rose an octave or four. "This isn't ending."

"You mean that?" I tilted my face back to look at him. He smiled, bright, wide, heart-stopping.

"Happily ever after," he said softly, capturing my lips with his.

Happily ever after. I could live with that.

"Are you ready for that?" he asked cautiously.

"More than ready."

"I don't want to rush you. I mean you and Jack-ass just broke up, and I don't want—"

I pinched his lips closed to shut him up. "Jack and I were never together," I admitted. It was as though a weight had been lifted from my shoulders. The relief I felt from being unburdened by that lie was refreshing. I felt lighter.

"What?" His eyebrows pulled together in confusion.

"Jack is gay. He's my best friend, other than Bailey."

"Gay! Jack is gay?" He couldn't disguise the shock in his voice if he tried.

"Yep." I watched with amusement as he processed what I'd told him.

"So the kisses and the touchy-feely?"

"Meant nothing. To either of us." Though I had a feeling Jack enjoyed himself just a bit.

"And you and he have never—" He cleared his

170

throat. "Never shared a bed?"

"Oh, we've totally done that. A lot, actually." I couldn't help it; I liked making him squirm.

His face paled, and his mouth set in a firm line. "Just to sleep, right? Please tell me you've only ever slept beside and not *with* him," he pleaded with fear reflected in his eyes.

"Only to sleep. In fact, I build a pillow wall between us, so he stays on his side of the bed."

"Good, but you know this stops. Now."

"Of course."

"But..." I could see the wheels turning in his brain while he tried to figure everything out. "He said you were...he still kissed you, groped you, treated you like shit."

"He did." I nodded.

"Why?"

"His plan was to make you so crazy jealous that you stepped in and swept me off my feet, declaring your love for me in some big, grand gesture. He has a flair for the dramatic."

"Well, he was right. I've been going crazy these last few days watching you two together. They were going to put you and Jack in the adjoining rooms, but I convinced Nate and the desk clerk to put me and you together. I wanted to keep as much distance between you two as possible." He chuckled, bringing one hand up and tracing the curve of my neck. His fingers left a trail of goose bumps on my overheated flesh.

"Really? Why?"

"I was jealous from the moment he introduced himself as your boyfriend and wanted you all to

171

myself as often as possible."

"Good. I'm glad."

"Glad about what?" His hands drifted over my shoulders and down my arms, making me shiver.

"About you being jealous. Now you know how I felt. An eye for an eye, and all that."

"How you felt?"

"Do you think I enjoyed coming home for Cole's birthday, only to find out you were engaged? Why do you think I haven't been home since?" As much as it hurt at the time, it was good to admit all this to him. I felt like telling him everything would give us a clean slate.

"That…that was the biggest mistake I'd ever made and a story for another time." He pressed a kiss to my lips. "Do you want to go back to the dinner? It's only early."

"I guess we should." I nodded and pushed myself up to stand.

"Wait." Linc's hands dusted the sand of the back of my skirt. "This is nice. I can do this whenever I want now without looking like a creep." He laughed and jumped to his feet.

"We better go back and do some damage control." I slid my hand into his, smiling when he brought it up to place a kiss on my knuckles.

CHAPTER TWENTY

Linc

It was a night of confessions, and I couldn't have been more thrilled with the way things went. I was glad for whatever fight Indie and Jack had that forced her to admit her feelings, because I couldn't keep going the way I had been. It was driving me crazy watching her with Jack and not being able to tell her all the things I wanted to or hold her the way I was right then.

We were in the elevator, and Indie had her arms wrapped around my waist, head pressed to my chest. I was sure she could hear my heart beating a million times a minute. It had been since she called me a stupid ass and told me she was in love with me. It was something I had hoped would happen, but nothing could have prepared me for how I felt when she said those words.

The elevator doors opened, and she reluctantly pulled out of my arms with a sad smile and walked toward the ballroom. I liked that she was as disappointed as I was that we had to go back to acting like nothing was different once we went back into the rehearsal dinner. But we weren't through those heavy oak doors yet.

I reached for Indie's hand and pulled her to the corner of the hallway.

"Linc," she shrieked when I pushed her up against the wall. If anyone was to come out, I hoped the potted plant beside us provided enough cover.

"Shh." I brushed a strand of hair out of her face and traced her lips with a finger, watching as her mouth pulled into a smile.

"What are you doing?" Her chest was rising and falling rapidly, and there was slight pink tinge to her cheeks.

"This." My voice was low and quiet, grazing my mouth against hers and trailing kisses along her jaw. Her lips parted, and a small sigh escaped.

"Linc," she breathed, her tongue darting out to wet her lips, and I couldn't resist. I slanted my mouth over hers. I wanted to devour her. I didn't think I'd ever get sick of kissing Indie. Everything about her was perfect. The way her hands ran up my back and into my hair, pulling on my dreadlocks. The way she moaned when I pulled her bottom lip into my mouth. The way she smiled at me like I was the only person on the planet she wanted see.

"As much as I want to continue this, we'd better go." I pulled away with a frown.

"You're right." Indie nodded before stepping forward and wrapping her hands around my neck, pulling me in for another kiss.

"Like kissing me, huh?" I smiled playfully.

"You have no idea." She sighed dreamily and pushed me away, then strode toward the door. "Are you coming, stupid ass?" She shot a wink at me over her shoulder.

"We're going to have a chat about this newfound nickname one of these days, Princess." I scowled and pushed the door open for her.

"Whatever. You love it." She patted me on the chest and breezed into the room as though everything was great, which I guessed it was.

For now, everything was perfect. It was when we had to sit down and tell her family we were...what were we? We hadn't discussed it, exactly, only that it was a forever thing. So did that mean she was my girlfriend? I watched as Indie strolled over to the table where everyone was sitting. Bailey jumped up immediately and pulled her into the chair beside her, smoothing out the kinks in hair her from where my fingers were tangled only two minutes earlier. Bailey appeared to be asking a lot of questions, constantly shooting glances at me, but Indie continued to shake her head, refusing to say anything.

Nate walked over to me. "She good?"

Yeah, man, she was exquisite. "Yeah, she's fine."

"Good. I don't know what happened earlier, but whatever you said, she looks happy again."

"She and Jack broke up." I tried to hide my elation. I didn't know why I told him that. Maybe to gauge his reaction.

"Good. They weren't right for each other, anyway." He nodded and walked off.

Joining the table, I noticed Indie was talking with her parents, so I interrupted briefly to apologise for the scene we caused earlier, but they reassured me everything was fine—they were used to our outbursts. We did tend to fight a lot, but in hindsight, it was most likely more out of frustration at bottling up our feelings. At least, on my part it was.

I pulled out a chair and sat with Ryder and Brody, pouring myself a drink. Jack was sitting across from me with a curious expression on his face. His eyes kept drifting from me to Indie and back again. I knew he caught me staring at her more than once because, frankly, I couldn't take my eyes off her now. And I didn't want to.

"Dance with me?" Bailey suddenly asked Ryder.

"You know I don't dance, baby." He shook his head, eyes narrowed and lip ring pulled into his mouth. I'd come to realise that was pretty much his look all the time. Happy. Pissed off. It was always the same.

"Come on, Jones. Practice for tomorrow night." Bailey pouted and fluttered her eyelids. Damn, she was good. I was about to offer to dance with her.

Ryder groaned. "You know I can't say no to that face."

"I know." She jumped up and grabbed his hands and pulled him onto the empty dance floor.

I couldn't help but laugh, because I knew I'd be the exact same with Indie as Ryder was with Bailey.

Whipped.

But I didn't care, and I had a feeling he didn't care in the slightest, either.

"Kenz, another practice run?" Nate asked, leaning on the back of my chair.

"Got nothing better to do. Just keep your hands off my ass." She tapped his ass and followed him to the middle of the room.

"Ahh jeez. It's my turn, isn't it?" Brody sighed and tilted his head back to look at the ceiling.

"Looks like it." I laughed and leaned back in my chair.

"Indie—" Brody called.

"Indie is dancing with me." I cut him off, earning a chuckle from him and Jack. "We need to practice for tomorrow," I said, hoping they'd believe it, but I knew they wouldn't. Brody had figured out my feelings for Indie somewhere along the way. Hell, even Jack had figured it out, and that was before I'd met him, so I had no doubt they knew something was going on with Indie and me now. I could only hope neither of them was stupid enough to tell anyone yet.

"In?" I called down the table.

"Sure." She kissed her parents on the cheeks and headed my way. "Keep it classy, yeah?"

"Of course. I am nothing but class." I took her hand and led her onto the dance floor. I knew I'd be trying to find any excuse to touch her in some way from now on. But that was okay; I liked a challenge.

It was only a matter of minutes before Brody and Harper joined us, and that only left Jack sitting at the table alone. I felt bad for him. He looked bored and maybe a little down. It was hard to tell. He'd been so loud and annoying these last few days that I couldn't tell what was really good acting or what was him.

"You should go and talk to him," I said softly in Indie's ear, nodding in Jack's direction.

"Yeah, I know, but…"

"But?"

"I kind of want to stay here with you."

My heart swelled, filling my chest. I smiled and turned her away before leaning in and whispering I'd be back in the room waiting for her. I wasn't going to sit awkwardly and watch everyone else. I was going back to the room alone to wait for her to join me. "Go." I gave her a gentle shove then went to say goodnight to Leanne and Steve, who said they were leaving as well.

Shouting a goodbye to everyone else, I left the ballroom and took the lift to the eighth floor.

I had a shower to freshen up and make sure I smelled good when Indie returned. I wanted to impress her.

She called me "stupid ass."

I ordered a bottle of wine because my nerves were getting the best of me, and I didn't know how to handle that. I'd never been nervous around her before.

She loved me.

I sat on the balcony, the fresh air calming me down a little and clearing my mind. There was nothing to be nervous about.

I was in love with her.

I paced the room restlessly. I didn't like waiting. What if she was having second thoughts?

No, she was in love with me.

I checked Indie's room.

Where was she?

I lay on the bed.

She was coming back, right?

I went back into her room, grabbed her suitcase and all the things from her bathroom, and brought them back into my room.

She had to come back.

And then there was a knock at the door.

She was back.

I rushed over, smoothed my hands over my hair, adjusted my pants, and opened the door, expecting to see Indie. I frowned. It was Jack.

"Can we talk?" he asked.

"Sure, I guess." I stepped aside to let him in.

He gripped the neck of my t-shirt, twisting it between his fingers, and shoved me against the wall. What the hell was his problem?

"I'm going to say this once, and only once," he seethed in my face.

I nodded. I believed he was serious and knew I would have done the same thing had the roles been reversed. Hell, I had done the same thing. Numerous times over the years.

"You hurt her, and I'll cut your balls off and use them for golf practice," he said. "Understand?"

"Understood." I nodded.

Jack smiled, released his grip on my shirt, and patted me on the chest. "He's all yours, baby cakes," he called over his shoulder.

Indie walked into the room with a nervous expression on her face. "Thanks."

"Anything for you." He kissed her on the cheeks and fluffed her hair before turning to me. "Oh, and one more thing."

"What?" I was unsure if I really wanted to know.

"How do you rate her kisses?"

"Jack!" Indie groaned.

"Rate her kisses?" I crossed my arms over my chest.

"Yes, from an A-plus to an F. Like school," He grinned excitedly.

Indie covered her face with her hands and sank to the floor.

I didn't know where he was going with that question and why she looked so mortified, but I intended to answer truthfully.

"Because I gave her a solid C," he declared. "What about you?"

He gave her a C? A C? He couldn't be serious. Indie's kisses were so much more than a C. They made my knees weak and my pulse race. They had me wishing I could kiss her forever. Indie's kisses were definitely an "A-fucking-plus. Her kisses are ace."

Indie's head shot up, and she stared at me wide-eyed.

"Wow, she's really improved. Just remember, I taught her everything she knows." Jack grinned widely and walked into the hallway. My fists clenched, and I may have growled. "You can thank me later," he sang as he walked down the hall.

"He didn't teach me. I swear we only kissed those few times that you saw. That's all." Indie jumped to her feet in an effort to explain.

"Shut up," I said and kicked the door closed.

"Linc?" Her eyes were wide, fearful.

180

She shouldn't be afraid. For every step I took forward, she moved back one, until she hit the wall.

"I want to know every single place he kissed you. I want to know every part of your body he touched. I want to know everything." I placed my hands on the wall beside her head.

"Linc?" Her pout drew into a frown.

"You're mine. I'm going to kiss you until Jack's kisses are nothing more than a black hole in your memory. I'm going to feel you, caress you, whisper across your skin until Jack's touch is erased from your body entirely. Do you understand?" I kept my tone even, letting my lips graze her ear, relishing the fact she shivered from my words alone.

"Y-y-yes."

CHAPTER TWENTY-ONE

Indie

Fuck.

He wasn't lying. Not by a longshot. I wasn't sure how much more I could take. It was torture. Pure torture. And it was divine.

Linc pulled me into his chest and kissed me until I could no longer stand before sweeping me into his arms and carrying me to the bed, where he proceeded to remove my dress at an incredibly relaxed pace. He stood back and pulled his shirt over his head, exposing his toned abs. What I wouldn't do to trace my tongue around each and every defined muscle on his body. My mouth watered just thinking about it.

He stood in front of me, unbuckled his belt, and slipped his pants down, kicking them to the side. And there we were, standing face to face in nothing but our underwear. I wanted to wrap a blanket around me, but it was definitely not the time to get self-conscious. He'd seen me dressed like this more than once over the last few days. But something in his eyes made me nervous.

"You're beautiful, Indie." He walked around and came to a stop behind me. He twisted my hair to the side and placed a kiss on the top my shoulder, dragging his lips across my skin and up the side of my neck to my ear, flicking my earlobe with his tongue, and my eyes rolled back in my head. His breath was hot on my neck. His hands caressed my arms, my stomach, my back. I felt him everywhere. His presence was such a force that I was surrounded by him. His scent, his touch, his warmth, his body.

"Did he touch you here?" Linc skimmed his hands across my stomach.

"N-no," I barely managed to choke out. His fingers ignited a fire in my belly.

"Here?" My ribs.

"No," I breathed.

He moved his hands to my back, over my shoulder blades, down my spine to the top of my underwear. Gliding his hands across my lower back, he asked again, and this time I nodded. Linc dropped to his knees behind me. I stiffened immediately. What was he doing? But one kiss on my lower back from his soft lips, and all thoughts left my head. His mouth torched my skin, his teeth grazing as he kissed the width of my back.

He was killing me. Painfully. Slowly.

His hands dropped lower, tracing the edge of my underwear, skimming over the fabric and the curve of my ass. "Here?"

"Y-yes." I didn't know what he was going to do. My stomach rolled with nerves and anticipation. Everything was so intense and full on. I was on high alert.

He gripped the waistband of my lace briefs and lowered them about an inch before placing one light kiss on the top of each cheek. Dragging his hands down my legs to my feet, he pulled them back up at a leisurely pace. He was taking his time, exploring my body and setting my nerve endings alight.

"Have I missed anywhere else?" he asked softly, pulling himself to his feet behind me. I expected him to move back in front of me, but he didn't.

I shook my head. It was a lie. But I wasn't sure I could handle any more of his touch, his kisses, and his close inspection of my body.

"Are you lying?"

Damn him for knowing me so well. He could always tell, growing up, when I wasn't telling the truth.

The bed creaked, then his fingers dug into my hips and spun me to face him. He was sitting on the edge of the mattress.

"Are you lying?" He pulled me forward until I was sitting on his legs, my knees on either side of him, my hands on his shoulders for balance.

"Where else, Indie?" He wrapped his arms around my back.

I pointed to my neck, angling my head to the side. Linc's lips descended and met with my overheated skin, kissing, nibbling, sucking until I couldn't take any more, and I moaned. His lips were magical. They had to be.

"Is that it?" he asked, tucking my hair behind my ears, a look of adoration on his face. A look that was hard to believe was directed at me.

"No," I sighed, biting my lip nervously.

"Where?" Linc held his hand out between us. His jaw was clenched, his eyes dark. I knew he wasn't liking the fact Jack had touched me so often. "Show me."

Taking a deep, calming breath, I brought a shaky hand to his wrist and lowered it until his hand was cupping one breast.

He raised an eyebrow in question, and my silence was all the answer he needed. A deep, low growl rumbled from his chest. "He's a dead man."

Soft and gentle, he explored my chest, cupping and squeezing and massaging, his eyes never leaving mine. My breath caught in my throat, and my head fell back. He kissed down the column of my throat, dragging his lips down my chest and tracing the swell of my breast with his tongue before doing the same to the other. My insides liquified. If it weren't for his hand on my back, supporting my weight, I would have collapsed in a heap.

"Tell me again. Has Jack touched you anywhere else?" he demanded, his hands back on my hips, his stormy grey eyes penetrating mine.

"Jack who?" I mumbled, still able to feel his touch everywhere.

"Good girl." He brought his mouth down on mine. Gripping my hips harder, he lifted and shifted me to the side, lowering me until I was lying back on the pillow, with him above me, never once breaking the kiss.

We were in an intimate position. A position I knew led to other things. Things I wanted with Linc but wasn't sure I was ready for yet. Butterflies erupted in my stomach, and my hands trembled. He could still make me a nervous wreck, but it was Linc. I shouldn't have been nervous.

"You're shaking. Why are you shaking?" He broke our kiss and pulled back slightly, holding my trembling hands to his chest. "Are you cold?"

"No." I shook my head. "Just nervous, I guess."

"Why? There's no need to be nervous." He smiled and placed a soft kiss on my forehead. "I've got you."

"Just…I've never—" I trailed off, embarrassed. I knew it wasn't something to be ashamed of, being a virgin, but it didn't stop the doubt creeping in. He had been engaged to a stripper, for goodness' sake, and I'd only ever kissed two people, and one of them was gay.

"I know. And we're not going to do that."

"We're not?" My eyes narrowed, and my mouth dropped. I didn't even wonder how he knew. He didn't know what I did while at uni. The door to my bedroom could have been revolving. All I focused on was he said *no*. He didn't want me that way? Was something wrong with me?

"Oh, no! Ace, come on. We are definitely doing that. I can't wait to do that with you. Forever. We're just not doing it now. Tonight. I want to wait until after we've told everyone," he clarified. Relief washed over me. I wasn't un-wantable, after all. "Tonight, I just want to kiss you senseless. We have a lifetime of missed kisses to catch up on, and I'm starting now." He lowered his face to mine and captured my lips with his again.

Pulling back, I smiled. "You called me Ace?"

"A-fucking-plus." He kissed me again.

"I like it. Ace and stupid ass. Has a nice ring to it, don't you think? Though we could just shorten it to ass." I laughed.

He rolled his eyes and shook his head in disbelief. "Can you shut up, so I can get back to kissing my girlfriend, please?"

My heart stopped, and my breath caught in my throat. "Girlfriend?"

"Well, yeah. You sure as hell aren't my sister."

"Thanks goodness for that. But I'm your girlfriend?" I wanted to hear him confirm it once more. This was the moment I had been waiting for my entire life. This was what had filled my dreams for as long as I could remember.

"Yes. I figured 'happily ever after' kind of implied that." He traced a finger down the bridge of my nose.

"So, what are you waiting for, boyfriend? Kiss me senseless." I closed my eyes, wrapped my arms around his neck, and puckered my lips, doing a great impression of a fish.

"Girlfriends are bossy. Maybe I need to rethink things." He smiled against my lips.

CHAPTER TWENTY-TWO

Linc

The early morning sunlight filtered through the gap in the curtains, but we'd been awake for hours, lying in bed enjoying our time together. It was the day of the wedding, so we were making the most of being alone. The moment we stepped out of this room, we had to go back to pretending we were nothing more than friends.

I wasn't sure I could do that. Looking back, I didn't think we were ever just friends. And I didn't want to pretend we were. Not now that I knew what it felt like to touch her and kiss her whenever I wanted. Not now that I knew what it felt like to hold her in my arms all night, knowing she loved me.

I never wanted to let go.

"Can I ask you something?" Indie lifted her head from my chest, her fingers dancing across my collarbone.

"Anything." I twirled her hair between my fingers and focused on her eyes. Her emotions were on full display, and the seriousness in her tone had me worried.

"Can I lick your collarbone?" She grinned playfully.

"What?" I couldn't contain my laughter. That was not what I was expecting her to ask.

She shrugged. "You have a really pretty collarbone."

"Pretty?" I raised an eyebrow. There was nothing pretty about me. I was a man. And men weren't pretty.

"Manly." She narrowed her eyes and deepened her voice to imitate a guy. "Rugged."

I was still laughing.

"Look, it's just really sexy." She slapped my chest and tried to pull away.

"You can lick whatever you'd like, Ace." I smirked and brought my hands up, folding them behind my head. "Have at it."

Her eyes widened, and she sat up, curling her knees under her. With her bottom lip pulled between her teeth, she dragged her gaze from my face and down my chest.

"What's wrong, In?"

"You're making fun of me, aren't you? You don't think I'll do it," she said, lying back down beside me.

"I'm still waiting." She was right. I didn't think she'd do it.

She propped herself up on her elbows and raised a challenging eyebrow.

"Go on, then." I nodded, giving her my permission to lick my collarbone, and dammit, she did.

Not in a sexy way. Not in the way I hoped she would. No, she stuck her tongue out and dragged it across my skin, just once, like she was licking an ice cream, and hell if it still didn't make my toes curl.

She smiled at me, one hundred percent proud of herself. "Proved you wrong." She giggled.

"Yes, you did." I laughed and hugged her to my chest.

She snuggled against me and sighed.

"What's up, Princess? Want to lick my funny bone now?"

"That's not even a real bone."

"I know. What are you thinking about?"

"Jasmine…"

"Indie, that's—"

"I know you said it was a story for another time, but I want know. Please tell me."

I couldn't say no to her. Me getting engaged to Jasmine culminated in Indie avoiding me, her family, and coming home for over a year. I owed her an explanation.

"Okay." I groaned and wiggled down in the bed a little more to get comfortable. Indie's hand rested on my heart, and I was sure she'd feel it beating in its cage. "I met Jasmine a while ago. About six months before Cole's birthday—the last time you came home. There wasn't anything particularly special about her. We didn't connect at all. It was just physical…"

She tensed in my arms.

"Sorry, Ace, but I don't want to lie to you." I kissed the top of her head.

"Okay," she whispered.

"She was just there at the right time. I used her as much as she used me."

"How?"

"When I met her, I was hurt. In more ways than one. I'd just been released from hospital, and I was heartbroken over...you."

"Me?"

"Let me finish. Jasmine danced—literally—into my life when I was feeling low. I convinced myself that I needed to get over you, move on, and she was there, willing. She didn't care that my heart wasn't in it, that I didn't love her and never would. She just wanted someone to take care of her. Someone who could support her enough that she could finish her degree and quit stripping for good. So we got engaged. But I couldn't do it. No matter how hard I tried, I couldn't erase you from my thoughts, from my heart. I guess you were my bad habit too, and I knew without a doubt I'd never be able to quit you either. I called the whole thing off. And you should have seen my parents. I don't think they'd ever been so happy about anything in their lives. It seemed no one thought Jasmine and I should get married, but no one wanted to tell me to my face."

She was silent. I didn't know if that was a good thing or a bad thing. Panic set in. What was she thinking? Did this change her feelings for me? What—

"You said you were in hospital. Why didn't I

191

know about that?"

"You didn't?" She didn't know I was unconscious for three days. She didn't know she was the first person I asked for when I woke up, and the nurse stared at me blankly, not knowing what I was talking about.

"Of course not. If I had, I would have been there in a second. Sat beside you until you were allowed to go home. It wasn't serious, was it?"

"I had a car accident. Lost control in the rain because I was driving so fast. Spent a week in hospital, three days of which I was out completely. But I was okay. I thought—" Dammit, everything I'd thought was wrong.

"What?" Indie sniffed.

"I thought you knew and you didn't care that I was hurt. Every day I was in that hospital, I waited for you to come running through the doors. And every day you didn't show up, it broke my heart, until I decided enough was enough and it was time to move on."

Indie lifted her head and looked at me with tears in her eyes. "Linc, I'm so sorry. I never meant to hurt you. I really didn't know." She choked back a sob.

"Don't cry. It's okay. It's all worked out now. It took us while, but we finally got our shit together."

"How did I not know? Did Nate and my parents know?"

"Hospital called your mum first because they couldn't reach my parents. They were there with me every day."

"No one thought to tell me? I would have been

right there, probably chained myself to your bed or something. Nothing would have made me leave without knowing you were okay." Tears were streaming down her face.

"Come here," I said and pulled her up until her nose brushed mine. "None of that matters now. It's all in the past. What matters is us, here, now, and the future. I love you." I brushed a strand of hair behind her ear and tilted my lips up to meet hers.

"I love you too, you stupid ass. Don't get in any other car accidents. I couldn't bear it."

"Okay, I'll try." I chuckled. Her nickname was growing on me.

"No more speeding. Nothing is so important that you have to break the road rules and risk your life to get there, Lincoln," she scolded.

"You were."

"Me?"

"I was chasing after you. Remember you'd come home for a week because you had a break from classes, but we had a fight. I can't even remember what the fight was about now, but you packed your bags and got the next flight out. I decided in that moment I couldn't let you leave, not without telling you how I felt."

"Stupid ass," she said before kissing me again. And again. And again.

CHAPTER TWENTY-THREE

Indie

The day flew by. There was so much to do before a wedding. My mother had us booked in for manicures and pedicures. Lavenia had hired someone to come and do our hair and makeup. We had to make sure the guests who were flying in today were settled in quickly. There was a photographer hovering around my mum's suite, taking pictures of everything and everyone as they were getting ready. A steady supply of champagne, thanks to room service, kept us in high spirits.

It had been nine hours since I saw Linc, and I missed him. I didn't know how I was going to get through the rest of the night without pulling him into a closet and kissing his beautiful face. It was like dangling a beer in front of an alcoholic and saying, "No, you can't drink it." Cruel. Torture. Awful.

The guys were doing guy things with my dad, which I was pretty sure meant they were having beers in the bar until it was time for the ceremony.

I helped my mum into her dress and almost cried. I'd never been to a wedding before, and seeing how beautiful and radiant my mum looked and how excited she was to be marrying my dad again made me wonder whether I'd have that. I loved Linc, and I'd be lying if I said I didn't dream about marrying him too, one day in the future, but I was worried. Not because I didn't think he would want to marry me—he did propose to Jasmine, and he didn't even love her—but because I didn't know how my family would react when they found out we were together.

We'd always been friends. My parents treated him as if he were one of the family. He was Nate's best mate, and there were rules about things like that, some sort of bro code. Dating your best friend's sister was high up on the "a bro shall not" list. The last thing I wanted to do was ruin their friendship.

We decided to tell everyone tomorrow over breakfast. In a public restaurant. Lots of witnesses. And plenty of exits, should we need a quick escape. I hoped we didn't. I'd like to think my parents would be happy for me...for us. They adored Linc and knew how much he cared and looked out for me.

"You ready?" Bailey asked, interrupting my thoughts. I was on the balcony getting some air. The ceremony was starting soon, so we had to get moving, otherwise the bride would be more than fashionably late.

"Yep." I forced a smile and walked back inside to where my mum and Lavenia were waiting. Kenzie and Harper slid their shoes off, throwing them into the bag Lavenia was carrying for all of us. The wedding ceremony was on the beach, so we were walking down the aisle barefoot. I took a moment to look at my reflection in the mirror beside the elevators and fix my hair, which was curled to perfection and pinned over one shoulder. I couldn't recreate the style if I tried.

We took the elevator down and made our way through the resort to the beach, catching people's attention as we went. A bride tended to do that. Stepping onto the sand, I was blown away. It looked magical. The sun was just setting. A long white carpet formed the aisle between the rows of chairs and led to the front where there was an arbour covered in greenery.

Nate waited off to the side, hidden by a wall of tropical plants and white silk, looking handsome as ever in his grey suit with white shirt buttoned loosely. "Ladies, you look lovely." He smiled at Bailey, Kenzie, and Harper. "Your seats are waiting for you."

They thanked him and gave my mum a kiss before heading to the front to watch the wedding. There were so many people seated. I didn't know she invited this many.

"Looking good, In," Nate said before turning to kiss Mum on the cheek. "And you look beautiful. Ready to do this? You know, it's not too late if you're having second thoughts and want to back out."

"Oh, Nathaniel, don't be silly. I've wanted this my entire life." She smiled up at him. "Now, let's get this wedding started." She linked her arm through Nate's and prepared to go.

"Wait!"

"What, sweetie?"

"Where's Linc? I can't walk down there by myself."

"Right here, Ace," he called from behind me, making my heart beat a little harder and my breath catch in my throat. I turned cautiously to see him and froze. Nothing would work. Nothing would move. My chest tightened, and my lungs burned from lack of oxygen.

"Oh, Lincoln, don't you look divine?" my mother gushed. "Doesn't he look wonderful, Indie?"

Ummm…

My brain had short-circuited.

"Indie, you okay?" Linc looked entertained. "You're turning blue."

I was glad he was amused.

"Take a breath, Princess." He reached out and brushed a curl behind my ear.

I gasped, sucking in as much air as I could and placing a hand over my heart to calm it down.

"There we go. Hi," he said, smiling softly at me, his grey eyes sparkling.

"Hi," I said a little too breathlessly. Had Mum and Nate noticed I was acting weird? I didn't care, really. Not when Linc stood before me looking like that.

He was wearing the same pale grey suit as Nate, with the white shirt that was open at the top. But he rendered me speechless. There was something about him in a suit that drove me crazy. He'd kept the scruff on his face, but he had it trimmed, accentuating that jawline. His hair was pulled back into a ponytail at the back of his head, with a large grey band holding it in place. But it was his eyes that got me. They were solely focused on me.

"You look beautiful." His hand was still in my hair as he leaned forward and brushed his lips against my cheek. I pouted and would have stomped my foot too had my brother and mum not been watching. I wanted to kiss him. I wanted to drag him into the bushes and rip the buttons off his shirt.

"You don't look too bad yourself, stupid ass." I tried to play it cool and act like I wasn't undressing him with my eyes as I reached up and fixed his collar. It didn't need fixing. It was just an excuse to touch him a little more.

"Indie. You did not just call Lincoln a stupid ass. That's very immature. I'm so sorry, Lincoln," Mum scolded.

"It's fine, really." He brushed it off with a smile. He liked it when I called him that. And in my own weird way, I guessed I was telling him I loved him without risking someone hearing. It was like our own secret code. Ace and stupid ass. We were so romantic.

"Okay, well, let's get this wedding started," Nate announced and clapped his hands twice.

A string quartet—she hired a freaking string quartet—started playing the Wedding March.

"Indie?" Linc held his elbow out for me, allowing me to wrap my arm around his.

We walked down the aisle toward my father, who rocked back and forth on the balls of his feet nervously, just like I did when I was nervous. Everyone rose to watch as my mother was escorted by Nate.

It was a beautiful moment. I hoped one day my dad would walk me down the aisle and proudly hand me over to Linc, whose eyes still had not left me, not even for a second.

The ceremony was short, but it didn't need to be long. They said their vows and exchanged new rings, and that was it. Once all the guests had left the beach for the ballroom, the photographer wanted to get some photos of my parents, so we were excused and allowed to go up to the reception.

"You look gorgeous, baby cakes." Jack came over and gave me a kiss on the cheek, much to the annoyance of Linc, if his growl was anything to go by.

"Man, I can't wait to get out of this suit," Nate complained, tugging on his collar as though he were wearing a tie.

As we passed the doors to the main foyer, Linc nudged my ribs with his elbow and tilted his head toward the door while discreetly pointing to Nate.

"Oh, damn. You know what? I think I left my room key upstairs. If I don't get it, I won't be able to get back in later. Think you can let me in so I can get it?" I asked Linc, stopping by the doors.

"Yeah, I guess," he said casually.

"Want us to wait?" Nate asked.

"I'm sure they can find the ballroom on their own," Kenzie said. "They're grown-ups, after all."

"You sure?" Nate asked again.

"Yeah, go. It's fine. We won't be long."

Nate nodded and walked off with Jack and Kenzie. Everyone else had already gone to the reception, so we were alone.

"Come with me." Linc grabbed my hand and dragged me over to the corner, mostly out of sight from passers-by.

Pressing me against the wall, his mouth came down on mine. His fingers dug into my hips while mine slipped inside his shirt and traced along his collarbone. I really did like that bone. I sighed into his mouth, allowing him to slide his tongue against mine. I'd been wanting to do this all day.

"This is driving me crazy," he hissed against my lips. "It's been one day, and all I can think about is you. Talking to you, touching you, kissing you. I don't like this hiding, Indie."

"Neither do I. Tomorrow. We'll tell them tomorrow." I leaned forward and pulled his lip between my teeth, making him groan.

"You better not have learned that from Jack," he said, pressing his forehead against mine.

"Way to ruin the moment, stupid ass." I slapped his chest and pushed him away, and he laughed.

"Yeah, I love you too." He chuckled as we turned around and came face to face with my parents.

Oops.

CHAPTER
TWENTY-FOUR

Linc

The entire night was tense. I could barely dance with Indie when I was supposed to. I couldn't look at her. And I sure as hell couldn't look at her parents. They busted us kissing in a dark corner, and it immediately made me feel like I was back in high school. The look on the Kellermans' faces nearly killed me. Shock. Anger. Disappointment. I never wanted them to be disappointed in me, let alone Indie. Was it really that bad if we were together? The idea that they thought so little of me, that they wouldn't approve of Indie and me, was devastating.

I spent as much time with my parents as I possibly could. They'd flown in that morning and were flying back tonight because my dad had a big case he was working on and couldn't afford to take the time off. I was surprised they even made the trip, but I was grateful to them for doing so. Having them here gave me a reason to avoid everyone else, when all I wanted to do was speak to Indie.

"Something's wrong, honey." My mum patted my cheek in that caring way she did and gave me a half smile the moment Dad excused himself to the bathroom. "Did you and Indie have a fight?"

"What? No. Of course not. Nothing's wrong. Why would you even ask that?" She had always been perceptive. Even growing up, she always knew when I'd done something I didn't want her to know about. Like the time I snuck Indie into my room when she was seventeen because she'd had too much to drink, and I couldn't risk her parents finding out. Mum knew.

Like each and every time I scared off one of the losers who wanted to date her, give her flowers, touch her ass. Mum knew.

Like the time I got engaged to Jasmine because I was trying to get over a broken heart. Mum knew.

"I'm not stupid, Lincoln. I have eyes, and that girl over there," she pointed at Indie making her way around the room, talking to guests with a forced smile, "has not stopped looking at you since you both walked in here, but this time she doesn't look happy like she usually is when she sees you. This time she looks like she wants to cry."

Dammit. I clenched my jaw. I didn't want her to cry. There was nothing I hated more than Indie feeling sad. But I couldn't have this discussion with my mother right now without speaking to Indie's parents first.

"Everything is fine." Yeah, that sounded

believable. I rolled my eyes at myself.

"Lincoln Andrews, don't you dare lie to me," my mother scolded. She hadn't used that voice on me since I dragged mud through the house after getting caught in the rain while helping Nate and his dad build a shed in the back yard.

I caught Indie's eye and smiled, but she didn't return it. She really was scared. I wanted nothing more than to go over there and hug her and tell her it would be okay, promise her everything would work out. I knew she hadn't spoken to her parents much tonight either, choosing to be overly social and not stay in one place for more than a minute or two. Yeah, my eyes hadn't left her either.

"I screwed up, and I don't know how to make it right." I sighed and looked at my mum for advice, even though she had no idea what happened. How could I fix the disappointment in the Kellermans' eyes? How could I turn back time and not have dragged Indie into that corner?

"I'm going to ask you something, and I want an honest answer." She reached forward and clasped my hands between hers. I nodded.

"Do you love her?" she asked softly. I couldn't process how she would even know that. I was too shocked.

I nodded. Of course. I always had.

She smiled, wide and bright, and let out a little laugh.

I guessed that made her happy. If only Indie's parents had the same reaction.

"Enough to risk losing Nate as a friend?"

I nodded again, because it was no contest. I

loved Nate. He'd always been there, but I was in love with Indie. Everything was about her. It always had been.

"Can you walk out of this room and never see her again?"

"Hell, no." I clenched my fists between Mum's hands, making her release me. There was no way I could walk away from her. I'd fight hell and high water to keep her beside me.

"Then you need to go over there and make sure that girl knows, no matter what, you're not giving up."

"How? I mean…how?" I glanced at Indie again; she was still watching me. How could I reassure her that we were in this together, no matter what?

"You're a smart boy. You'll figure it out," Mum said.

"How did you know? I never told anyone how I felt."

"I'm your mother. I know these things. Now, go!" She gave my shoulders a light push.

She knew these things. Maybe I hadn't been as good at hiding my feelings as I thought. After all, Brody had worked it out too. I stood and hesitated. I didn't know what the hell to do.

"Go big, or go home. That's what I always say," Mum said encouragingly.

"You've never once said that." I raised my eyebrow in disbelief.

"I am now."

Taking a deep breath and letting it out gently, I turned to face Indie. There must have been something on my face that revealed my intentions, even if I didn't know them myself, because she stopped her conversation with one of her uncles and took a step toward me, her hands twisting together in front of her. She looked so damn beautiful in that dress, biting her bottom lip in nervous anticipation.

Nate appeared in front me. "Hey, man. Can I talk to you about something?"

"Not right now," I said and sidestepped him.

"But it's—"

"Sorry, I have something important to do." I walked away before pausing and turning back to him. "Can you just not beat the shit out of me until after the reception?"

I really didn't want to ruin his parents' wedding day, and a fist fight between their son and his best mate over their daughter would absolutely do that.

"Okay," he said slowly, a look of confusion on his face.

I spun on my heel and marched directly to Indie, not giving much thought to anything or anyone other than wanting to see her happy smile once more.

Screw it.

"Linc," she breathed as I got closer. My body crashed into hers as I grabbed her face between my hands and kissed her. For a moment, everything else faded away, and it was just us. Her body warm and soft against mine, her hands around my neck and fingers twisting into my hair.

"Go big, or go home," I breathed against her mouth.

"What?" She chuckled.

"Nothing." I kissed her again, quickly. Too

afraid to let her go and too terrified to turn around and see everyone's reactions, I rested my forehead against hers. "Everything is going to be okay, yeah?"

"But—"

"No buts. It will be fine." It had to be fine; I wasn't losing her.

"Okay."

"Ready?"

She sniffed and nodded, her eyes wide with fright, but I figured if Nate hadn't smashed my head through a table yet, maybe it wasn't going to be so bad. Or he was making good on his promise to not beat the shit out of me until after the reception.

I didn't know what I expected when we pulled apart and looked around the room, but it wasn't the reaction we got. Well, lack of reaction, rather.

Indie released a breath slowly and looked at me with one eyebrow raised in question. I shrugged in response because I didn't know how to answer.

No one even spared us a glance, except for my mother, who was smiling into her wine glass. But no one else cared. No one saw. No one said anything.

CHAPTER TWENTY-FIVE

Indie

Had we completely misjudged the reaction we'd receive? Did no one even care that Linc had just kissed me in the middle of the ballroom? Surely someone would have seen and made a comment about it.

Linc's fingers threaded through mine. I smiled at him nervously, still not accepting the fact no one actually cared.

The unmistakable sound of the heavy ballroom door opening echoed through the room. I looked over, catching a glimpse of Nate storming out just as they slammed shut behind him. Someone definitely saw. That was the reaction I had been waiting for.

"I better go and speak to him." Linc pressed a kiss to the side of my head and released my hand.

"Not without me." I reached for his arm,

207

gripping it tight, and walked with him to the doors. Bailey caught my eye on the way out and gave me an excited two thumbs up with a big smile on her face. Jack sat beside her looking like the cat that got the cream. He shot me a wink as Linc and I stepped through the doors.

The hallway was empty. Nate couldn't have gotten that far unless he ran. I looked at Linc as he ran his hands through his hair nervously.

"Where'd he go?" I asked.

A thumping sound came from around the corner. We approached slowly, peering around the edge of the wall where we saw Nate kicking the baseboard with his shiny, pointed black shoes.

"Dammit." He muttered a string of curse words that would make a sailor blush.

"Nate." I stepped forward, only to be held back by Linc, with him positioning himself in front of me. For protection? From Nate? Nate would never hurt me. I was his sister. We looked out for each other.

His eyes flicked between Linc and me. I couldn't read the expression on his face.

"You." He pointed at Linc. "You did this."

He charged for Linc, grabbing his shirt in his fists, and shoved him into the wall behind us.

"This is your fault. You played me for a fool," he seethed at Linc.

I closed my eyes, terrified he was going to hurt him.

"Nate, stop. Please," I begged, reaching out to pull his arm off Linc.

"Step back, Ace. He's right to do this. I expected

it." Linc's voice was so subdued.

"Do what?"

"Break my nose. Do your worst, brother. I deserve it."

I couldn't watch. I could not watch my brother beat up his best friend. There had to be a better way. Couldn't he see Linc and I were perfect for each other?

"Nate?" I said again but stopped when he began laughing.

He released Linc and smoothed down his shirt, still laughing. "I'm not going to break your nose." His eyes focused on me. "Yet. But if your hurt her, I can't be held accountable for my actions. Got it?"

"Loud and clear. Don't worry, I don't plan on hurting her." Linc smiled then came over and wrapped an arm around my waist.

"Well, what was that all about, then?" I gestured to the wall Nate just had Linc pinned against.

"I lost the bet." Nate groaned and kicked the wall again.

"What bet?" I narrowed my eyes and crossed my arms in front of me.

"Jack bet me that you two would get your acts together and finally hook up by the wedding. I, however, bet against him, sure it wouldn't happen because I've been waiting years for you two shits to stop dancing around each other and finally bite the bullet." He rubbed his hands over his face.

"You knew?" I gasped.

"How?" Linc asked at the same time.

"You guys were so obvious. You." He pointed at Linc. "Always fixing your hair and straightening your clothes whenever Indie walked into a room, preening like a god damn kitten." He laughed. "And, Indie, I've never known anyone try so hard at sport and fail, continuously, over the years so this idiot would keep teaching you. And don't get me started on the scary movies. Newsflash, you both hate horror films, yet you both watched them all the time, just so you could end up curled up together on the couch." He placed his hand over his heart. "Sweet. Touching. Really."

I couldn't believe he knew. All this time.

"How much?" Linc asked.

"What?"

"How much did you lose to Jack-ass?"

"Stop calling him Jack-ass. It's not nice. And it's not true." I stomped my foot.

"Sorry, Ace. The name stays, at least for now."

"Stupid ass," I mumbled, and Linc grinned. "How much did you bet Jack?"

"Five."

"Five bucks? That's it?" I breathed a sigh of relief that it wasn't more. Nate had a tendency to exaggerate sometimes, but he shook his head.

"Five hundred dollars," he groaned. My mouth dropped open in shock.

"Sucks to be you, man." Linc laughed and started leading me back to the ballroom.

"You can split it with me," Nate said, jogging to catch up.

"Hell, no. That's your fault for trying to make money off me and your sister." He paused with one hand on the door handle and looked at Nate. "So, we're all good?"

"Yeah, we're all good, unless..."

"I hurt her, but it won't happen, because I plan on making her my wife." Linc grinned and pushed the doors open.

My mouth dropped open.

"Close your mouth, Ace. You're drooling." He tapped my chin with his finger.

"Stupid ass," I mumbled, still trying to wrap my head around the whole *wife* comment.

Linc winked at me and walked off.

"You're really okay with this?" I asked Nate.

"Yes. I'm just surprised it took you both this long." He stood beside me with his arms crossed.

"We both thought you'd freak out."

"Well, if it was anyone else, I might have, but it's Linc. He's loved you forever, and he's always done right by you. He's a good guy."

"He really is," I agreed. "Can I ask you something though?"

"Sure."

"Why didn't you tell me about his accident?" I didn't know what made me think of it, but I was suddenly curious why they would keep it from me.

Nate ran a hand over his face and sighed. "You'd left pretty mad. I wanted you to have a few days to cool off before I called you, but then he was fine, and I didn't see the point in worrying you over nothing. Or stressing him out when he needed time to recover. Sorry, sis. I should have told you, but I was looking out for you both."

"I guess that makes sense. Still not happy I only just found out, but it's in the past," I said, falling silent as my gaze met Linc's.

"You happy?" Nate asked.

"Yeah." I sighed dreamily as I watched Linc talking to my parents. He was intense, his hands waving around, and whatever he was saying appeared to have the desired effect. My mother hugged him, and my dad shook his hand, clapping him on the back and pulling him in for one of those awkward man hugs.

"What was that?" I asked when he came back over and pressed a kiss to my lips.

"That's my cue to leave." Nate cleared his throat and looked away, pretending to see something interesting on the other side of the room and leaving us alone.

"That was me speaking to your parents." Linc wrapped his arms around my waist and started swaying to the music.

"About what?"

"Us."

"What about us?"

"Just told them that as much as I tried not to, I love you and want to spend the rest of my life with you."

"And?" I asked hopefully.

"What more do you want?" he teased. "I asked your dad for permission to marry you," he said casually, like it was no big deal.

"You did what?" I screeched, pulling back.

"He said yes. Seemed like he couldn't wait to give you away. Do you irritate your folks that much?" He laughed.

"He said yes?" I was shocked. After the look on their faces earlier, I was prepared for a war.

"Seems like they knew as well. Apparently, everyone knew but us."

"So, we're getting married. Is that what you're telling me?" I asked as Linc grabbed my hands and pushed me out, spinning me under his arm and bringing me back in again. When did he learn to dance like that?

"Not so fast, Ace. I haven't proposed...yet." He brought his lips down to mine.

CHAPTER TWENTY-SIX

Linc

There was a party after the reception that I was really keen on skipping. I had a girlfriend I wanted to spend as much time alone with as possible. But things rarely worked out the way I'd hoped. The after party somehow ended up occurring in our room. Well, Indie's room, because Jack-ass had the key and let everyone in, but the connecting door meant my room was open for all as well.

It had probably been the most stressful night I'd ever had. Nate being okay with me and Indie meant a lot. The fact that he had known for years and hadn't said anything was surprising, though. If it had been the other way around, I would have been pissed, then I'd have come around and dealt with it and probably ended up teasing him about it constantly. But all he said was, "About time," and that was it.

The fact that Nate had been so cool about it gave me the confidence to speak to their parents. I wasn't nearly as nervous as I had been earlier when I was convinced I was a dead man. And again, they surprised me. Sure, they were a little disappointed they had to find out by catching us hiding in a corner, but they understood our hesitation at announcing it straight away, and after I reassured them I had her best interests at heart, and I intended to marry her one day, they were thrilled.

All that lying to ourselves and everyone else, all that sneaking around and petty games, and it was all for nothing. We had nothing to worry about at all. Everyone was happy for us. They'd taken bets, for crying out loud, on when we'd get together officially. Jack had taken that bet with more than just Nate, and if my calculations were correct, he was about two grand richer right now, which might explain all the champagne he ordered from room service. He had better be fixing up that bill when we checked out.

Indie's laughter floated across the room, catching my attention immediately. She was giggling at something Kenzie had said, and I stood mesmerised by her and her smile.

"So, how does it feel?" Brody came and stood beside me.

"What?"

"Being whipped." He laughed.

"Feels like I got the girl. Finally." I smiled at Indie, who had noticed I was watching her.

"Took you long enough."

"Yeah, yeah, I know." I shrugged, not really

caring that it took a long time. I had a lifetime to make up for the time we missed.

"Harper and I have been talking again," Brody murmured.

"Again? What do you mean?"

"Geez, man, you've been living under a rock this week. Or is it because I don't wear a skirt and go by the name of Indie that you don't pay any attention to me?" He shook his head.

"Sorry, I have been kind of preoccupied. Tell me what you mean by 'again.'"

"If you paid attention, you would have known Harper and I dated a few years ago, back when she was just starting at uni, but for whatever reasons, it didn't work out. After a while, she moved back to Blackhill, and I stayed in the city to finish my degree."

"You guys dated and broke up. How did we not know about this?" I didn't remember him having a girlfriend while away at school.

"Nate knew."

"Of course, he did." Nate knew everything, didn't he? "So?"

"So, what?"

"You and Harper?"

"Nah, man, nothing. It was just weird running into her here of all places after so long," Brody said, walking away.

"Right," I said with a nod. I was pretty sure there was more to the story, but I really didn't care. I just wanted to kick everyone out and get Indie all to myself, but instead, I followed Brody out to the balcony where the guys were hanging around drinking beers.

The sun was almost up when everyone decided to call it a night and go back to their rooms. Indie was tidying up the room when I grabbed her hand and dragged her out the door.

"Linc, what are we doing?" she whispered as we rushed down the hallway to the elevators.

"I want to see something," I said, pushing her in the elevator and kissing her quickly.

Once the elevator reached the bottom floor, I led Indie outside and to the beach, where I collapsed on the sand and pulled her down with me.

"What—" she began to ask, but I cut her off with a kiss.

"Just watch."

We sat quietly on the warm sand and watched the sun gradually rise on the horizon. "I wanted to see the sunrise at least once while being here." I pressed a kiss to the top of her shoulder. "But every morning, I've been too preoccupied with watching you sleep that I've always missed it."

"Sorry about that," she teased.

"I'm not. I enjoyed myself."

"This is nice. I wish this week didn't have to end," she said quietly, leaning her head back on my shoulder.

"Me too. But we've got more than this week together." I tightened my arms around her waist.

"No, we don't. I leave for uni in a couple of days and don't graduate for months."

"We've waited fifteen years for this, Indie. A few months won't kill us." I hoped I was right but feared I couldn't be more wrong. Sure, we'd waited fifteen years, but now I had her in my arms and in my bed, I didn't think I could let go.

"I'll come home every holiday and weekend," she insisted.

"And I'll come to you every other weekend and holiday. We can do this, Ace." I was determined to do this. I wouldn't let distance ruin us. I gazed at the horizon as the first sliver of light appeared over the water. "Look." I pointed at the sunrise. The sky was a blend of pink, purple, and orange.

Indie was quiet as we watched the sun, and I knew it was because she was thinking about what leaving here meant for us. I let her think, knowing she'd speak when she was ready.

"It's beautiful. Thank you for bringing me out here," she said after a while.

"Anytime, Ace. Come on. Let's go to bed."

CHAPTER TWENTY-SEVEN

Indie

I was going to throw up, I was so nervous. What if things didn't go the way I hoped? What if I made a fool of myself and he realised this was all a mistake?

What if?

What if?

What if?

"Will you relax?" Bailey said as she ran the brush through my hair one more time.

"I can't. I'm so nervous. I don't know how to do this." Butterflies erupted in my stomach, making the queasy feeling all the worse.

"You don't have to do anything. It will all fall into place, okay? Trust me?"

"She's right, baby cakes. All you gotta do is wear this, and everything will work itself out," Jack said, entering the bathroom with something

219

scrunched in his hands.

"What is that?" I cringed because I was almost certain I didn't want to know the answer.

"Lingerie, of course." Jack waved the flimsy black fabric in my face.

"I am not wearing that," I insisted, snatching it out of his hands and throwing it on the counter.

"Yes, you are. Tell her, B." He folded his arms over his chest and leaned against the wall. I was beginning to regret calling in reinforcements for this, but the truth was I need all the help I could get. We only had one night left in paradise, then it was on a plane and back to reality. And reality really seemed to suck, all of a sudden. Reality meant Linc and I would be hours apart until I graduated. It meant a long-distance relationship and lots of phone calls. It meant rushed visits on the weekends when we had a spare minute to see each other. It meant being alone, again, for the majority of the time. It also meant this was our last night together for who knew how long.

"I mean, I'm pretty sure you could wear a potato sack and Linc would still throw you down and boink your brains out, but—"

"Boink?" I laughed.

"He's right, Indie. You need to wear that. It'll blow his mind." Bailey agreed with Jack. Traitorous bitch.

"Okay. Fine. Get out." I ushered them out of the room and changed into the black lingerie. It was cute and sexy. Black lace underwear with a matching black lace baby doll-style top. I discarded the fishnets and the stiletto heels Jack had tried to persuade me to wear earlier and opted for a bathrobe to hide myself until the time was right.

Jack and Bailey were waiting for me when I returned to the room.

"You ready?" Bailey asked.

"I think so." I bit my nails. I shouldn't be nervous. This was what I wanted.

"Can't say I'm not a little disappointed that I won't be the one cashing in." Jack sighed dramatically. "But you know where I am if you need me." He kissed me on the cheek and walked out with Bailey, leaving me alone.

I paced the entire room thirty-three times before Linc came back from his surf. But the moment I saw him, all the nerves disappeared. This was it. The moment. Everything had led to this point in time. There was no going back after this, and I was more than ready.

"Hey, Ace." He smiled and kissed me quickly.

"Stupid ass," I greeted him in return.

"I'm just going to have a quick shower, okay?"

"Okay." The moment the bathroom door closed, I slipped off the robe so I was only wearing the lingerie Jack had picked.

The door opened three seconds later, and Linc came rushing into the room. The sound of water from the shower filling the room. "What's with these?" He was holding the stilettos and fishnets in his hand when his eyes landed on me. "Ace?"

"Yes?" I stood still, unsure of what to do next as his gaze swept over my entire body, his grey eyes darkening. He looked like he was warring with himself.

"Indie." His voice was low, a growl, and sent chills down my spine. "You have three seconds to change your mind and get dressed before I do something I've wanted to do for a long time." He spoke slowly and deliberately, giving me a chance to back out, but I wasn't going to. I wanted this.

"One."

He closed the distance between us in three long strides. I wasn't backing down.

"Two."

His hands found their way into my hair as he tilted my head and kissed the column of my throat. I wanted this.

"Three."

He growled, his hands dropping from my hair and tugging the lace top over my head. I was ready for this.

"So fucking perfect," he whispered as he brought his mouth down on mine. Slow. Passionate. Intense.

All thoughts of the running shower were lost immediately.

My knees buckled, and Linc caught me. He carried me and placed me on my feet in front of the bed. My body was overheating, desire flooding my veins. I wanted nothing more than him, to give myself to him. Right here. Right now.

"Last chance," he said, his lips brushing mine as his hands skimmed the waistband of my underwear, hovering there for a moment, and when I didn't respond, he ripped them off.

Oh my God. I was naked. Completely naked in front of a man. No one had ever seen me without my clothes on before, and the thought of that should freak me out and have me running from the room. But I wasn't freaking out. I was cool, calm, and collected...and, holy hell, what was he doing?

He pushed himself up and stood back. He looked at me. Why was he looking at me like that? Like I was the most precious thing in the world. I was naked, and he was standing there in his shorts, looking at me. He gripped the waistband of his board shorts, and I stopped breathing. Eyes wide, I stared at him, focused only on his face. I couldn't look anywhere else as he dropped his shorts and stepped out of them.

My traitorous eyes lowered...lower and lower. Oh my God, he was naked. Completely naked in front of me. I'd never seen a man naked before, and...I was totally freaking out. I fell back onto the mattress quite ungracefully.

What was I supposed to do now? With him? With his—? It was right there. Umm...

"Ace, you okay?"

I tried to respond. I tried to nod, to open my mouth, anything, but I couldn't function.

"Shit." He dropped to his knees in front of me, his hands framing my face. "Ace? It's okay. We don't have to—"

I lunged for him. Something snapped in my brain, and I lunged for him. Wrapping my arms around his neck and crushing my mouth to his, we tumbled to the floor. I needed to kiss him. I needed to do something other than stare at his, umm...him. Oh, geez, he was naked underneath me. I could feel him pressed against me. Everything.

Pushing that thought aside because it would only

make me panic, I allowed myself to get lost in his kisses and the way he held me to his chest like he couldn't get me close enough. His hands trailed up my back and wove through my hair, angling my head so he could deepen the kiss. I moaned. His kisses were that good. Our tongues danced together, fighting for dominance while our bodies remained pressed together in very intimate places.

Linc rolled to the side, sliding me off him, and gave me a moment to regain my composure before he climbed to his feet once again. He reached down to me and pulled me up to stand in front of him. His chest rose and fell as rapidly as my own.

"Shower," I blurted.

"What?" His eyebrows furrowed as he bit his bottom lip.

"The shower is still on. Shouldn't you—" I said absently because his hands were roaming my body again, tickling my hips, my stomach, my ribs. "Turn...Turn it—"

He walked me backwards until my knees hit the bed.

"What?" His lips were on my neck, sucking gently. Hands firmly gripped my hips and pulled me into him and his...

My breath caught in my throat. Hell, I could feel him, right there between us. And it was...I didn't know what it was, but it was there.

"Off. Turn it—" Again, his hands distracted me, moving up and brushing over my breasts.

"I'd much rather focus on you right now, Ace," he said into my shoulder before gently lowering me onto the bed and stretching his body out beside me.

"I want you to stay still. Think you can do that?"

I shook my head and said, "Yes." Then nodded and tried again. "No." I didn't know what I could. My hands were trembling again, and my breathing was erratic at best.

"Do you trust me?"

"Yes," I whispered.

"So, relax." He brought one of my hands up between us and kissed the pads of each finger before repeating on the other. It was such a sweet and tender moment that emotions bubbled away, threatening to spill over in the form of tears, but I held them back.

He kissed behind my ear and dragged his lips down my neck, grazing my collarbone and over my chest until his mouth was on my breast. What was he doing? Was he? Was that his...? His tongue. Sliding. Gliding. Swirling. Lips. Teeth. Teeth? I tensed, but one touch from his hand over my heart told me to calm down. It was Linc; he wouldn't bite me.

His glorious mouth continued its assault on my body, wreaking havoc on my nerves as he kissed and licked and nibbled, down my ribs, across my stomach, over my hips, the inside of my thighs.

The inside of my thighs.

I jerked my legs, but he held me still. He was too close. Was he going to kiss—? Lick? Nibble? No, that would be too weird. Right?

Sensing my thoughts, he lifted his head and smirked at me. "Not today, Ace, but one day."

My eyes bugged out of my head. He skimmed his mouth down my calf before moving to the other leg and gliding all the way back up, over my hips, across my stomach, past my ribs, and focusing his attention on my other breast.

Was it hot?

It was definitely hot. Maybe we should open the doors and let a breeze in, or maybe—

He slid his body over mine and kissed me slowly and with so much passion I thought I was going to burst into flames. His kisses calmed me down. My nerves settled, and I felt safe. Secure. Loved.

He slipped his hand between us, and his fingers moved in a...

Whoa. My eyes rolled into the back of my head. Everything tingled. Everything was on fire. Everything was screaming at me for *more*.

"More?" he asked, kissing my jaw.

Dammit, I said that out loud.

"Yes," I breathed, clutching his back.

"Are you sure? We can wait."

"Now." I grabbed his face and brought his lips to mine again.

"Now," he repeated, before freezing. "Dammit!"

"What?" I brushed a dreadlock out his face.

"I don't have a condom." He groaned and dropped his head to my chest.

"You don't?"

"No. Well, I didn't plan on seducing you this week, did I?" His lips pressed into my skin just above my rapidly pounding heart.

"Pretty sure I seduced you, you stupid ass."

He looked up at me with flint in his eyes. "You have no idea."

My eyes widened in shock. I seduced him? "I

did?"

"Hell, yes. You were always either wet, in your underwear, or both. That does things to a man, Ace."

"I'm on birth control," I announced rather quickly, my thighs parting a little more.

Linc grinned and settled himself between my legs. "Thank God for that."

His mouth met mine as he pushed into me gradually. And...ouch.

I gasped, tensed my muscles, and screwed my face up. That hurt. It was not at all like the movies or Bailey's romance novels. No way.

"I'm sorry, Princess. Want to stop?"

I shook my head, still squeezing my eyes and digging my nails into his back. If I had to feel pain, then so did he. It was only fair.

Each time he moved inside me, Linc placed gentle kisses on my jaw, my nose, my tightly squeezed eyes, between my eyebrows, and my lips. He kissed me softly, sweetly, and with so much tenderness I could have cried. But that might have been the incredibly uncomfortable feeling I was experiencing.

He moved leisurely and carefully, with such a gentleness, as though afraid he'd hurt me, and didn't stop kissing me until the uncomfortable feeling start to subside, and...Oh!

CHAPTER TWENTY-EIGHT

Linc

She was perfect. She was everything.

And I didn't think I could say goodbye tomorrow. Not now. Not after being with her. Worshipping her. Her body. Loving her until we both fell asleep in a mess of tangled limbs. Her body fit mine flawlessly. The saying that two people were made for each always seemed like absolute shit until now. Indie was made for me.

I woke some time during the night, not because I was tired, but because I couldn't stop thinking about the following day. The sun would be up too soon, and that meant we only had a short time together before it was time to part ways.

I was going to do everything in my power to see her every weekend. She would only be a few hours away, and it was only for another six months until she graduated. Once she was finished with school, we could plan our future. As long as I had the surf and Indie, I didn't need anything else.

I traced my fingers lightly down her spine and across her back. In the moonlight, I could just make out the light dusting of freckles on her nose, her eyelashes casting a shadow on her pink cheeks. Her lips were still slightly puffy from kissing for so long, but I couldn't get enough of her.

Her breathing increased, and her arm tightened around my waist. She was awake. She slid her leg between mine and pressed a kiss to my chest before looking up at me with a sleepy smile. "Hi."

"Hi, Princess." I brushed her hair out of her face, rubbing my thumb across her cheek and lips.

"Why are you awake?" She pushed herself up until she was lying on top of me, her mouth millimetres from mine.

I wrapped my arms around her back and held her close. "Watching you." I rubbed my nose along hers and captured her mouth with mine when she sighed.

"What time is it?" she asked quietly.

I shook my head. "Sun will be up soon." My voice was subdued, and the light in her eyes dimmed as the reality of the situation sank in.

"Do we have to go?"

"Afraid so." I cupped her face and kissed her again, languidly exploring her mouth. She moved against me, her body soft and warm, her hips lined up with mine. I pulled back just enough to speak when I realised what she was doing. "Ace?"

"Please." Her lips moved against mine, our breath mingling.

I leaned forward, closing the tiny gap, joining

our mouths as I lifted her hips a fraction before helping her lower herself on me.

I swore I saw stars. Flashing lights. I might have even passed out. I would never get enough of her this way. Open. Trusting. Vulnerable. Mine.

***

We had a shower together. A long, hot, silent shower. No words were exchanged. The mood was very downcast. Indie was so lost in her own thoughts, she didn't even notice when I washed her hair and lathered her skin. She didn't notice when I shut off the water and wrapped her in a thick, fluffy towel, then dried her hair and her body.

I did get a small, grateful smile from her pretty mouth when I pulled the bathrobe on and tied it around her waist. We didn't need to speak, though. We'd said all the words we'd needed to. All the important ones. We'd spent an incredible night together, and now it was over. We had to leave for the airport in a few hours, and that would be it until one of us could make the trip to see the other.

Room service arrived, and we ate on the balcony like every other morning. Indie poured my coffee, while I filled her plate with pancakes and syrup and berries, just the way she liked. It seemed the hotel went the extra mile for us, today being our last day. But the silence was getting to me now. I wanted to know what was going through that gorgeous head of hers.

"Talk to me, Ace. What's up?" I asked, only to receive a blank stare. I climbed out of the chair and grabbed Indie by the hands, pulling her to her feet as well.

I wrapped my arms around her and held her tight, breathing in the scent of her hair, memorising how every curve felt pressed against mine. Her fingers dug into my back, and she buried her face in my chest.

"Indie, please? I've tried to be patient and give you time to think, but I can't cope with this silence any longer. What's wrong?" I tilted her face up to mine. Her eyes glistened with unshed tears.

"I don't want to say goodbye." She sniffed and bit her bottom lip to stop it from trembling.

"Hey, it's going to be okay."

"How do you know? You'll be home in Blackhill, and I'll be across the country at uni. What if you get tired of waiting? What if you change your mind? What if—"

I slammed my mouth down on hers. Gripping her hips, I lifted her and pressed her into the wall behind us. Her legs tightened around my waist, and she moaned into the kiss, while her fingers found their way into my hair.

"I," I said against her lips.

"Have." I skimmed my nose along her jaw.

"Waited." Kissed below her ear.

"Fifteen." Traced my tongue down her throat.

"Goddamn." Grazed my teeth over her collarbone.

"Years." And crashed my mouth against hers again, sliding between her parted lips. I kissed her until I couldn't kiss her anymore. I kissed her until we were both breathless and struggling for air.

"Nothing is going to take you away from me. I won't get bored. I won't change my mind, and I sure as hell won't give up on us. I already told you, we're getting married someday, Ace, so quit worrying and kiss me while we still have the chance."

"Stupid ass," she muttered then wiped a tear from her eyes and kissed me.

"Yeah, I love you too, Princess."

EPILOGUE

Indie

I couldn't wait any longer. It had been six very long months. I was packing my bags and heading home to Blackhill, a place where I belonged, and also a place I felt I'd outgrown. So much had changed this year. I was a completely different person, and I wasn't sure Blackhill was the place for me.

"I can't believe this is happening. I can't believe you're doing this to me. Please don't do this. Change your mind. Stay here with me. We could be happy together. I know I can make you happy, Ace. Just give me a chance."

"Will you quit calling me Ace?" I zipped up my suitcase and glanced around my room to make sure I had everything.

"Fine. Baby cakes, please don't leave me. You're my best friend." Jack threw himself on the ground at my feet and hugged my knees.

"Jack, get up."

He shook his head. "Not until you promise you'll stay."

I wiggled my legs and tried to get free of his hold, but I had no luck. He had a good grip.

"We will see each other all the time," I said. "I promise."

"You're lying. You'll get home with Adonis and forget all about me."

"Adonis?" Linc asked as he strolled through the door and took a seat on my bed.

"Yeah, handsome. You're Adonis," Jack mumbled, pushing my legs apart slightly so he could stick his head through and see Linc.

"Little help, please?" I looked over my shoulder at Linc and wiggled again in an attempt to dislodge Jack.

"Dude, we've spoken about this. Hands off my girl."

I liked when he got all possessive and called me *his*.

Jack sighed dramatically and let my legs go, before curling in a ball on the floor and rocking himself back and forth.

"What's wrong with him?" Ryder nodded at Jack as he walked into the room.

"We're leaving him behind. Where's Bailey?"

"Just checking the house again to make sure nothing is left behind." He crouched in front of Jack. "Man up. You'll graduate in six months, and then you'll be out of here too."

"But six months is a long time, and we're all going to be apart. I don't think I can do it. I mean, long-distance relationships never work. Someone always gets sick of waiting and cheats or breaks up with the other—" Jack rambled until Ryder slapped him over the back of the head.

"Idiot."

I stared at Linc.

"Ace, no. Don't even—" He reached for my hand and pulled me onto his lap. "No."

I knew he was telling the truth. I knew he'd never cheat. I wasn't insecure. I trusted him completely.

But it still didn't stop Jack from planting that tiny seed of doubt.

What if?

I needed to fix this soon. Erase the sliver of fear from my mind, and make sure that we got our happily ever after.

He wove his fingers through my hair and pulled my face to his. "No."

"I know." I pressed my forehead to his and breathed him in. It had been a month since I'd seen him last—the bi-annual surfing competition held on our beach in Blackhill did a great job at keeping him away, and I was so busy finalising everything here and preparing to move home while I looked for a job that time slipped away. "I've just missed you."

"Okay, we've got everything," Bailey announced as she came through the door. "Jack, what's wrong?"

I pulled back, and Linc released me so I could stand.

It was time to go.

Sadness washed over me, and I suddenly understood why Jack was curled on the floor that way. Everything was going to change now. Things were never going to be the same.

"It's going to be fine. You know you can always come to Blackhill when you finish, right?" Bailey reached out to pull him up. Jack looked at her and sniffed, a hopeful expression on his face. "You can stay with me and Ryder. We should have our own place by then, right, Jones?"

Ryder glared at her, but she smiled sweetly, knowing he wouldn't argue with her right now for the sake of getting out of here as soon as possible.

"Of course," he ground out through clenched teeth and a fake smile that lacked his trademark dimples.

"Really? You mean it?" Jack jumped up with enthusiasm. "Hear that, baby cakes? We'll see each other all the time." He scooped me into his arms and spun me around until I was giddy. I caught a glimpse of Linc's face as I twirled, and he didn't look impressed. I didn't think he'd forgiven Jack for treating me so badly back in Fiji and for kissing me when we weren't even dating.

"See, I told you it would all work out." I laughed, relieved that Jack had a renewed optimism.

He set me down on my feet. "Of course it would. I wasn't worried," he said, trying to play it cool.

"Uh-huh," Linc interrupted and came to stand behind me, sliding his hands around my waist. "We need to get going. It's getting late, and we've got a long drive." He placed a kiss on the top of my shoulder, causing a shiver to run up my spine.

Jack stood in front of us, eyes downcast and chewing on the corner of his bottom lip. A sad puppy dog had nothing on him. My heart broke. I really was going to miss him. Three years of friendship, all the ups and downs, living together, late night chats, dreaded shopping trips—he was the best person a girl could want as a friend. I lunged for him, pulling myself out of Linc's hold, and wrapped my arms around his waist.

I didn't even realise the tears were falling until Jack tipped my face up to look at him and wiped them away. "Aww, baby cakes. Don't cry. We'll see each other all the time. I promise." He tightened his arms around me and kissed the top of my head.

"But long-distance relationships are so hard, Jack. What if you forget about me?" I sniffled.

"Never. Going. To. Happen."

"Promise."

"Scout's honour."

"You never went to Scouts."

"I'll pinkie swear if I need to, baby cakes," he said, rubbing his hand comfortingly up and down my back, suddenly full of confidence. Two minutes ago, I had been comforting him.

"I believe you." I gave him a half smile. I couldn't muster a full one.

"Let's get you in the car and on your way," Jack said and grabbed my hand. He shot Linc a look over my shoulder, daring him to challenge him or say something about our hands, but Linc just gestured to the door and let us go out first.

The house was almost empty. Barren. A wasteland with all our stuff packed in boxes and loaded into the two trucks. Linc brought his own truck, and Ryder borrowed Jayden's, with Jayden

237

driving Ryder's car back to Blackhill for him. We had left Jack with enough furniture to get by. He was keeping all the big items, but without our personal touches, the place looked empty.

Outside, Jack shook Ryder's hand before pulling him into the awkward man hug for a little too long, making Ryder look uncomfortable, but I knew he was going to miss having him around. As much as Jack annoyed him, they were great friends. Bailey hugged him goodbye and promised he could stay with them when he came to visit or should he decide to move to Blackhill himself. I didn't think he would move there, though. He was too big a personality and too outgoing for a small town like ours. He'd do well in a big city where he had more opportunity to advance his acting career. We all knew he'd be a star one day. Acting was as natural as breathing to him.

Jack turned to Linc, and they glared at each other, mouths set in a firm lines and arms crossed as they seemed to be in some sort of standoff. Jack broke first, reaching out and shaking Linc's hand. "Look after my girl, or I'll hunt you down."

Linc smiled and nodded. "She's right with me. See ya, man."

And then it was my turn, and I really wasn't ready to say goodbye. I bit my bottom lip in an attempt to hold back the tears, but it was futile. There was no stopping them.

"I'm going to miss you most of all, baby cakes," Jack said softly, blinking rapidly to stop his own tears as he swept me into his arms for one last hug.

"Call me every day," I said into his chest. "And

if you can't call, I want text messages, emails. A letter. Send me a letter."

"Every day." He placed one last kiss on my forehead and let me go, pushing me into Linc's waiting arms. The tears were flowing freely. I couldn't even see as Linc led me to the car and helped with my seatbelt like I was a child, but I was shaking and too upset to do it myself.

"Love you," Jack said, blowing me a kiss just as Linc closed the door.

"You'll see him soon, Ace," Linc assured me once he was in the driver's seat beside me.

I couldn't speak, so I closed my eyes, not wanting to look at Jack as we drove away because I might have thrown myself out of the car to get back to him. I didn't think saying goodbye to him would be this hard, but it felt like I'd already lost him completely.

We drove in silence for the longest time, Linc's fingers threaded through mine and our hands resting on the console between us.

"How you doing over there?" he asked after a while, his voice startling me back to reality.

I shrugged. I didn't know how I was doing. I'd just said goodbye to my best friend and was moving back to my home town, without a job, without any sort of plan but to be with Linc. He was my plan. He was all I knew I wanted. All I had ever dreamed about, and now that dream was going to be a reality.

"Marry me?" I blurted out.

"What?" His head turned to face me, eyebrows raised in shock before he looked back at the road.

"Marry me?"

"That's not how this is supposed to work, Ace." He lifted our joined hands and pressed a kiss to my knuckles.

"You don't want to marry me?" My voice trembled. Had I gotten this all wrong?

Linc swerved to the side of the road and pulled the car to a stop. Ryder's truck sped past us as Linc turned off the ignition.

Grabbing my face in his hands, he forced me to look into his eyes. "Yes."

My heart dropped, and tears blurred my vision. Yes. He didn't want to marry me?

"I want nothing more than to make you my wife," he said, wiping away the tears on my cheeks with a gentle caress. "I just wanted to propose the right way, with a big gesture, be all romantic and stuff."

"Romance is overrated." I smiled through my tears.

He wanted to marry me.

"Say it again." He leaned his forehead against mine.

"Stupid ass?"

"Not that bit." His fingers wove into my hair.

"I love you."

"Ace?" His lips grazed over mine.

"Marry me?" I whispered.

"Yes," he breathed against my mouth before kissing me, his tongue sliding against mine. Long. Slow. Deep.

"Good answer," I mumbled and pulled him back for another kiss.

Sneak Peek

HARPER AND THE ONE-NIGHT STAND

Novel #3

R. LINDA

Coming Spring 2018 from Limitless Publishing

THEN

Harper

The thing about one-night stands is they're supposed to be just that.

One night.

One night of fun. One night of no strings. No commitment.

But sometimes a one-night stand won't go away. Sometimes a one-night stand keeps reoccurring, against your better judgement. Sometimes a one-night stand is just what you need, over and over again. But then it's not really a one-night stand anymore. Then it becomes something else entirely, even when you didn't want it to. It becomes something you can't walk away from, even though you know you should. Even though you know it can't continue without hurting someone else.

But sometimes...

You. Just. Can't. Walk. Away.

Sometimes you find yourself waking up in their bed when you should have been home alone in your own.

Sometimes you find yourself doing the walk of shame at the crack of dawn, attempting to sneak past their roommate's door before anyone finds out you were in the one place you both knew you shouldn't have been.

With my heels in my hands, I crept down the hallway that had become as familiar to me as my own, silently trying to escape before anyone woke up. The sun had barely risen, so I knew it was early. I should have felt guilty for sneaking out, but I knew even though it might hurt him to find his bed empty again, he'd understand. He didn't want this getting out of hand any more than I did. He didn't want anyone finding out about our…extracurricular activities any more than I.

We knew we were asking for trouble. We knew if we didn't stop this, it would blow up in our faces. And yet, we continued. There was something that kept bringing us back together. No matter how hard I tried to resist, all it took was one smile, and I was putty in his hands. But it was getting risky, and we really needed to stop.

"Don't forget your purse," Linc called from the kitchen. I froze, one foot on the fluffy grey rug, the other on the cold timber floorboards. Four more steps and I would have been free. Linc walked into the living room where I was contemplating running, with my purse in his hands. "Wouldn't want anyone to know you were here again last night, would we?"

Again?

I turned to face him, my fingers fiddling with the straps on my heels. "How long?"

"How long, what?" He raised a questioning eyebrow and threw my purse down on the coffee table beside me.

"How long have you known?"

He laughed and clapped his hands on his legs. "That it was you? About a month. That he'd been sneaking someone in here every couple of weeks? Since we got back from Fiji." He turned away from me and headed back into the kitchen. "Coffee?" he called over his shoulder.

My eyes widened, and I rushed after him into the small room, stopping on the other side of the counter. "Fiji was three months ago."

"Walls are thin, sunshine." He handed me a cup of black coffee and placed the smallest scoop of sugar into his.

My cheeks warmed in embarrassment. Oh God, he'd heard. I took a gulp of the liquid gold in my hands, scalding my throat, but I barely noticed. He'd heard.

"Don't worry. I have noise-cancelling headphones."

"You can't say anything," I pleaded, clutching the coffee cup to my chest. "To anyone."

"You're playing with fire, you know." He narrowed his gaze on me, bringing his mug to his lips and taking a long, slow sip of coffee.

"I know." I hoisted myself on the barstool at the counter and ran my hands through my hair. "But please don't say anything to anyone. I don't want anyone to get hurt."

It was only supposed to be one night. One night of too many drinks and waking up one morning in

Fiji to find myself in his bed with no memory of the night before.

He lifted a shoulder casually and leaned against the counter, facing me. "I'll be quiet."

"You will?" I sagged in relief.

"He's my mate. And I know exactly what it feels like to want the one person you know you shouldn't want, remember?" His smile was full of understanding, and in that moment, I knew Linc would keep our secret. At least for now. He'd secretly been in love with his best mate's younger sister almost their entire lives, so he understood the struggle and the need for silence.

"But I don't...It's not like—"

"I don't care what it's like. It's none of my business. But you need to...you both need to figure this shit out now, before either of you gets too attached and *anyone* else becomes collateral damage. If this is only something casual, end it now before you hurt either of them."

"I don't want to hurt them."

"Then you need to figure it out."

"Do you really think it'll hurt Brody?" Even asking the question, I knew I sounded like an insensitive ass. Of course, it would hurt him. And that was the last thing I wanted. But there was something about Nate Kellerman that had me coming back for more.

"His cousin sleeping with his ex-girlfriend?" He screwed his face up and nodded. "Yeah, it'll sting. Just a little."

Just a little.

It wouldn't hurt just a little. It would hurt a lot.

I needed to end this now. I didn't want to be the cause of anyone's pain.

"I'll end it." I sighed and lowered my head to the counter. I didn't want to hurt Brody or lead Nate on if I didn't know where this was going. Because, really, I didn't know what I wanted. I didn't want a relationship, but I liked the way Nate made me feel. "It's done. As soon as he wakes up, I'll tell him."

Linc didn't speak. He eyed me sceptically and nodded once before pouring his coffee down the sink. "Good."

And then he picked up his surfboard that was leaning against the wall in the corner and left. He left me sitting there alone, waiting for Nate to wake up so I could end whatever it was between us before things got any more out of control.

Acknowledgements:

First and foremost, I must thank my family, my partner and children for giving me the time to write this book and for understanding when I didn't go to bed until after midnight and woke up hours before everyone else just to write these words down.

My mum, for helping out with the kids when I needed more time to write, and for her top-notch writing advice and scene ideas, even if they didn't make the final cut.

The team at Limitless Publishing for giving me this opportunity and liking my work enough to publish a second book.

My amazing and very patient editor Lori Whitwam for putting up with my complete lack of organisation and inability to meet deadlines. It was tough, but we got there.

Deranged Doctor Designs for their incredible cover design and knowing exactly what I wanted when I didn't know I wanted it.

And my beautiful friend Fiona, once again our late-night chats, your words of encouragement, advice and allowing me to bounce ideas off you, not to mention your exceptional research skills, helped me in more ways than one with this book.

Thank you all.